BY YOSHINO ORIGUCHI
ILLUSTRATED BY Z-ton

Dione Nephilim

Lorna Arte

Kay Arte

Illy

Arahnia Taranterra
Arachnida

CONTENTS

MONSTER GIRL DOCTOR

VOLUME
2

MONSTER MUSUME NO OISHASAN VOLUME 2

© 2016 by Yoshino Origuchi
Illustrations by Z-ton
All rights reserved.

First published in Japan in 2016 by SHUEISHA Inc., Tokyo.
English translation rights arranged by SHUEISHA Inc.
through TOHAN CORPORATION, Tokyo.

Seven Seas books may be purchased in bulk for promotional,
educational, or business use. Please contact your local
bookseller or the Macmillan Corporate and Premium Sales
Department at 1-800-221-7945, extension 5442, or by
e-mail at MacmillanSpecialMarkets@macmillan.com.

Follow Seven Seas Entertainment online at
sevenseasentertainment.com.

TRANSLATION: David Musto
ADAPTATION: Ben Sloan
COPY EDITING: Marykate Jasper
COVER DESIGN: Nicky Lim
INTERIOR LAYOUT & DESIGN: Clay Gardner
PROOFREADER: Jade Gardner, Stephanie Cohen
LIGHT NOVEL EDITOR: Jenn Grunigen
PRODUCTION ASSISTANT: CK Russell
PRODUCTION MANAGER: Lissa Pattillo
EDITOR-IN-CHIEF: Adam Arnold
PUBLISHER: Jason DeAngelis

ISBN: 978-1-626927-40-7
Printed in Canada
First Printing: May 2018
10 9 8 7 6 5 4 3 2 1

MONSTER GIRL DOCTOR

VOLUME
2

STORY BY
Yoshino Origuchi

ILLUSTRATIONS BY
Z-ton

Seven Seas

Seven Seas Entertainment

The Centaur with a Sprain

THE INCLINED ROAD was utterly unlike the brick-paved streets of Lindworm. It had been formed after long years of people coming and going over it, trampling it into existence. Glenn Litbeit was only riding in a carriage, but with the violent jolting of the cart, he couldn't help bracing himself against the walls and stiffening his body.

He was grateful for the luxurious down cushions that covered the seats. With them, even a long journey over the mountain roads wouldn't bother him.

"Are you enjoying the ride, Doctor?" The question came in through the window from in front of the carriage.

"Y-yes... Thank you. It's been very pleasant."

"Please don't lie to me. This mountain road's a smidge... rough, in some places, even for a first-class carriage like this."

Glenn peeked his head out the window.

Pulling the horse-carriage was a female centaur. Tisalia

Scythia made good use of her large frame as she tugged them along the mountain path with firm and steady steps.

Still, it was a steep road. No matter how hardened her body was, Glenn was sure that carrying a passenger carriage up such a sloping path was difficult for her. Her exhaustion came through in her voice.

In front of Tisalia were her two attendants, Kay and Lorna. The two of them kicked aside rocks and took down tree branches to guide the carriage safely on its path forward. They both had quite a similar air about them, but Glenn was finally able to differentiate between the two of them...to a certain extent.

"You prepared such a luxurious carriage for us, too..."

"There isn't any hardship I won't undertake for you, Doctor! Well...that's what I'd like to say to show off, but really, the city carriages would quickly fall apart on a mountain road like this. I simply prepared the sturdiest high-quality carriage we had," Tisalia replied, her breath growing more and more labored.

Centaurs originally lived in grassy fields. While they were excellent at traversing flatlands, scaling mountain roads was more of a burden than they were used to.

"Nevertheless, no matter where it may be, Scythia Transportation shall safely, reliably, and quickly carry our customers to their destination! We'll be arriving at the harpy village soon. So, Doctor—oh, and Miss Sapphee—please bear with us just a little longer."

"Thank you for your help," Sapphee said from inside the carriage, thanking Tisalia for her hard work. The two of them usually quarreled with one another, but Sapphee wasn't looking to bicker with Tisalia while she was covered in sweat and hauling her up a mountain.

Glenn and the others continued up the slope to the summit of the Vivre Mountains.

For those who were familiar with the path, it was possible to make the round trip in one day, but that was because they had specialized equipment and training to do so. The ice vendors that went up to the summit to get their ice practically dashed up the mountain road, but that wasn't something just anyone could do.

The large carriage's hefty cargo, weighed down with Glenn's medical tools and other necessary items, meant that it took even longer to move up the path.

However, their destination wasn't the summit of the mountains, but the harpy village on the way to the summit. They would be arriving before the day was out, so the centaur princess and her two attendants were feeling very exhausted. Glenn hoped that they would be able to rest properly once they got to the village.

"Still," Sapphee added, "I can't believe that octo-woman's unreasonable requests ended up going this far... I've gone straight past anger—now I'm just astonished at her audacity." Sapphee cast her red eyes downwards and gave a loud sigh.

"I was just as surprised, too, you know. For her to just tell us to go to the harpy village and give them examinations out of the blue like that..."

The harpies had built a village in the middle of the Vivre Mountains, where they now lived.

It was an extremely ancient colony that had existed before the beginning of the war between mankind and monsters. From the harpies' perspective, the comparatively new city of Lindworm most likely seemed like something built by outsiders in their lands.

The harpies of the village flew down to Lindworm sometimes to acquire things that they could only find in town and bring them back to their village. In turn, they came to sell animal meat and wild vegetables that could only be harvested in the mountains. With this mutually advantageous relationship between the city and the village, the harpies and the city of Lindworm kept on good terms with one another.

"Illy...was it?" Glenn asked. "That girl's name."

"Well, it was pretty hectic back then. I don't remember clearly what her name was, but...yes, that's what Miss Kunai said. That harpy girl who had an impacted oviduct."

"I heard that she was taken in by the village, since she had nowhere to go."

Two months had passed since Dr. Glenn stopped a slave-trader plot that involved trafficking harpy eggs. As nothing more than a doctor, it had been impossible for Glenn to defeat the bandits himself, but with the help of many people, including Tisalia and Lulala, the captured harpies were rescued safely.

Even without being able to aid in the fight, thanks to Glenn's skill as a doctor, he had been able to deal with one of the harpy girls' impacted oviduct and safely induce her to lay the stuck eggs. According to Glenn's teacher Cthulhy, that harpy, Illy, was currently suffering from a different ailment.

"According to what Miss Cthulhy said, her feathers are falling out. Falling out so much that she's become unable to fly," Sapphee said.

"If that's true, then we have to do something," Glenn said. "We have to go up to the village for the regular exams anyway. Even without Dr. Cthulhy's orders, we'd probably have ended up climbing up here."

The harpy village did not have a doctor. There seemed to be an herbalist that also acted as a midwife, but they didn't have the talent available to handle more advanced treatments. There were some among the harpies who would fly down to Lindworm to get medical care, but for patients that were struck with a severe illness, Glenn or Cthulhy had to go up to the village directly to treat them.

It was with these objectives in mind that they had gone on this medical exam trip to the village. They had been fortunate, however, to receive help from Scythia Transportation.

The only daughter of the company's leader, Tisalia Scythia herself, had reached out to Glenn and Sapphee, offering to bring them up to the village. She told them she had her own business to conduct there and that, "It would be quite simple to bring the Doctor and Miss Sapphee along, as well. Ha ha ha!"

With the strength of Tisalia and her two attendants, Kay and Lorna, Glenn had been able to proceed up the mountain road without incident.

As easy as the trip had been, Glenn was sure that work was awaiting him once they arrived in the village. There were many other people besides Illy who needed a doctor—or rather, there was no doubt in his mind that as soon as everyone heard a doctor had arrived, the whole village would be anxious to complain to Glenn about all of their usual aches and pains.

"Mistress, should we switch out with you after all?" said one of Tisalia's attendants.

"Oh, Mistress—you've sweated so much…" said another.

Tisalia had been the only one pulling since they set out in the early morning, after all.

"I'm okay! Here's my opportunity to show off and have the doctor agree to be adopted into our family!"

"Your aspirations are truly splendid, but…"

"Will the young gentleman really be happy to have you covered in sweat after climbing up this mountain?"

Tisalia had her eye on Glenn as a possible marriage interview candidate, but naturally Glenn had no such intentions. If he accepted her offer, he wondered just how angry it would make Sapphee, who would glare at him with her snake-like gaze every time the centaurs' conversation turned in such a direction.

"I just need to hold out a little longer… Oh?"

The carriage stopped.

Glenn poked his head out, wondering what was wrong, when he saw that a landslide had blocked off the road ahead of them. Tisalia took her hands off the carriage's handle and braced the wheels. It appeared they were going to be stalled there for a while.

"And everything had been going so smoothly, too… Oh, well. Kay! Lorna!"

"Yes, Mistress."

"We shall hold here for a few moments."

The two excellent attendants had already fetched a shovel out from among the cargo loaded onto the carriage. Fortunately, it wasn't a large amount of earth piled up in front of them. It seemed that if everyone helped out, it wouldn't take that much time at all.

"Maybe it's because of a recent earthquake?" Tisalia mused. "I've heard this area experiences quite a lot of them."

"That just might be the case," Glenn said. "I'll help, too."

"I can't let you do that, Doctor. Please rest..."

Glenn took off his white coat and went to jump down from the carriage to help the centaurs clear the rubble, but—

At that moment, the carriage shook as though it were trying to jump up into the air.

"...?!"

"Earthquake!" Tisalia shouted. "Doctor, get down!"

Without even needing to be told, Glenn was already crouching down inside the carriage. It was one of Scythia Transportation's high-quality models, and as such, it wouldn't easily be broken—or so Glenn thought. It was no comfort to him, however, as the trembling earth was enough to send the carriage bouncing into the air.

Across from him, Sapphee also pressed her body low against the bottom of the carriage, which violently rattled and clattered back and forth as the earth itself rumbled and groaned. A cry sounded from outside. Glenn was unsure whether it had been Kay or Lorna.

"It's a big...one!" Sapphee groaned.

The people of Lindworm weren't accustomed to earthquakes. Glenn had grown up in an area known to have many, but even still, he grew tense from the force of the trembling earth. He wondered if Tisalia was doing all right outside of the carriage. While it may have been true that centaurs stood on four legs, Glenn felt that the tremors would be too much for even them to remain standing.

As Glenn waited for the quaking to subside, he hoped that the carriage wouldn't overturn—and that the quake wouldn't cause another landslide. Soon, the tremors and the rumbling of the earth calmed.

"Is it...over?"

It had been an odd earthquake. One large tremor, a groan-like rumbling—and then it stopped. Glenn wondered if it were just a foreshock of something more to come. Praying that wasn't the case, Glenn quickly stepped out of the carriage.

"Miss Tisalia! Are you all right?!"

"Y-yes...I'm fine."

Outside of the carriage, Tisalia was lying on the ground.

Right at her side were Kay and Lorna. Kay in particular was down flat, clinging to Tisalia.

"I was on the verge of falling, but the two of them protected me..."

Tisalia stood up, letting out a sigh of relief. Lorna quickly got up after her.

"...Kay?" Kay's partner Lorna furrowed her eyebrows.

Kay remained collapsed on the ground. She tried to stand up

using her back legs but quickly stumbled as if she were a newborn fawn.

"Ow!"

"Kay?"

She couldn't stand.

Glenn immediately rushed over to her. Her beautiful leg was covered with an unmarred chestnut coat, but it seemed she was unable to raise herself up onto it. It only took a second for him to recognize what had happened.

"It seems you've twisted your leg, Miss Kay."

Hearing this, Kay gave a troubled smile. Glenn thought that since she couldn't move, she must be unsure what to do.

"Doctor?" Lorna asked. "Kay's leg is...?"

"A sprain, or maybe a broken bone."

It appeared her leg had come under too much strain while protecting Tisalia. If it had just been twisted, that would be fine, but Glenn thought to himself that if the bones were broken, it would make recovery much more difficult.

"If possible, I'd like to keep her off her feet, but..."

They were right in the middle of the mountain road. On top of that, their path ahead was blocked by rocks and debris. Glenn would be able to give emergency first aid but would have to wait until they reached the harpy village to examine her properly.

"Can you walk, Miss Kay?"

"Of course, Doctor, this is nothing... Augh!"

As soon as she tried to stand, she grimaced in pain. She put on a brave face, but she was in no condition to walk.

"We'll have Miss Kay ride in the carriage... Sapphee and I can walk."

"Kay," Tisalia said, "I'm sorry, because of me..."

"It's okay. It's not your fault at all."

"But still..." Tisalia was acting uncharacteristically uneasy and flustered. It appeared that with her long-serving handmaiden injured, she was unable to keep her composure.

There was still some distance left until they reached the harpy village. Glenn thought if they could somehow carry Kay safely to the village, it would be fine, but—

"I found them! They're over here!" As Glenn worried, a voice fell over them.

"Huh?" Looking upwards, he saw a big set of wings.

"I found the doctor!" It was a man's voice. The owner of the wings plunged into a nosedive and landed directly in front of Glenn.

Standing in front of him was a male harpy with dark brown feathers. The man had been acting as the vanguard, and a number of harpies soon came down after him. Glenn wondered if they had been circling up overhead. There were both men and women among them, and all of them were all quite young.

The man that had come down first gave a deep bow.

"We've come to pick you up, Dr. Glenn. The same goes for the ladies of Scythia Transportation."

"P-pick us up?"

"Yes. The recent landslides have made this path impassible, so we thought you might have been having trouble. The village elder ordered the young people of the village to bring you up ourselves. Allow us to guide you there."

"That...would be a huge help."

It was more than Glenn could have hoped for.

"One of our group was injured in the earthquake just now. Can you bring her up to the village first?"

"With pleasure. Bring that over here!"

Everything went quickly after that.

The harpies used a big piece of linen they had readied in advance to create an impromptu cloth stretcher.

Harpies were a species of monster that had arms that were like the wings of a bird. They didn't have five fingers like humans, so Glenn thought that they would lack the necessary dexterity—but it seemed his worries were unfounded. The harpies bent their wings and hung the cloth from them. Unable to use five fingers to get the job done, they sometimes skillfully employed their mouths to tie the necessary knots together.

Tisalia and Lorna used their natural physical strength to place Kay on the stretcher. Then the harpies bound the rope ends of the cloth to their feet and began to flap their wings, quickly carrying Kay up above the tree line.

"Even if it takes three people to do it, it's quite amazing they can carry a centaur up that high," Glenn observed.

"The skies are our home. This is nothing." The harpy man gave a big, confident smile. "Now then, let's clear this debris. Put your backs into it! We can't have a single accident happen while the doctor is on the road!"

Giving a shout of agreement, the harpies all began clearing away the rubble. They were given commands to guide their work, and they all moved together in perfect order. Glenn thought it must have been the harsh mountain environment that their community lived in that bred such a level of cooperation.

Cooperation like theirs was something that he thought was missing in Lindworm, the city where monsters and humans from around the continent had gathered together. Its status as a crucible of different species and races meant that the people living in the town were surprisingly disconnected, which in turn allowed slave traders and other gangs of criminals to slip into the city.

"It looks like they are counting on you, Dr. Glenn." Without Glenn realizing it, Sapphee had gotten out of the carriage and whispered in his ear. "The harpies are working hard—they're counting on your skills, Doctor."

"I-I know."

"It looks like things will be hectic once we arrive." Sapphee giggled. They were busy back in Lindworm as well, but if the harpies were anticipating Glenn's arrival enough to come and meet him here, then what Sapphee was saying was likely true. He was a bit concerned about how things would proceed and wondered exactly how many patients were waiting for him.

"You'll be busy, too, Sapphee."

"Of course." She nodded calmly.

As he waited, Glenn scratched his head and took off his coat. He couldn't leave everything up to the harpies. Grabbing a shovel, he joined them in clearing away the rubble.

"Kay..." Tisalia was still looking up at the sky, her gaze locked in the direction her injured attendant had been flown off in. Glenn thought to himself that she was truly a great leader to be so worried about her handmaiden's well-being.

✗ ✗ ✗ ✗ ✗

The harpy village was halfway up the mountainside.

Here, the thick mounds of mountain snow finally melted and gave birth to a river. That river flowed all the way down into the city of Lindworm, where it became the canals of the famous Merrow Waterways. Yet even in the middle of the mountains, it was natural for there to be a settlement beside its waters.

The village was in a mountain valley, which had likely been carved out from the rock face by the flow of the river over many, many years. The bluffs on either side appeared very difficult to climb. If one were to head towards the mountain summit from the ground, the only path available was the slow and gradual road along the riverside.

Tucked between those bluffs at the bottom of the ravine was the harpy village.

"Welcome and thank you for coming," an elder harpy with a long beard greeted Glenn, leaning on his cane. He was the chief of the village. Both of the wings on his arms already hung low from his loss of strength, and they looked almost like the sleeves of the robe he was wearing. It seemed he had long lost the ability to fly freely through the skies like the younger harpies that had guided

Glenn and the others to the village. It was a condition often seen in elderly harpies.

However, the gleam in his eyes peeking out from underneath his wrinkles was sharp as an eagle's, and it revealed the presence and dignity that had united the harpies of the village.

"It seems one of your companions was injured."

"Yes. Where is she now?"

"In a building we have for guests, removed from the village. We prepared it as a temporary dwelling for you when we heard you would be visiting. If you bring your equipment there, you'll be able to start your examinations posthaste."

This was all a great help for Glenn.

It wasn't his first time visiting the village, and the elder was familiar with doctors coming to stay. The village's lack of a doctor meant the chief knew to greet a capable doctor of monster medicine like Glenn with courtesy. If his teacher Cthulhy had been the one to visit, he was sure an even warmer reception would have been waiting for her.

"Our village is not made of sturdy rock like the city of Lindworm is, so your dwelling and bed may be different from what you're used to, but I beg you to please bear with us during your stay."

"Not at all. It will surely be more than adequate for us."

From what Glenn could tell, most of the houses in the village were built from wood, with grass and straw-thatched roofs. It was something unheard of in Lindworm, but once he looked up at the walls of the steep bluffs along the river, it became clear why the harpies didn't make their houses from stone.

There were many small huts built into the side of the bluffs, as if they had been glued to the rock wall. The wooden houses had been constructed using small protrusions that jutted from the bluff as their foundations. The harpies flitted to and fro among the small huts built into the cliffside with ease, but anyone without wings would have found it impossible to get into any of the houses. Built into the side of a cliff as it was, this village was obviously made for those who could fly through the air.

Glenn casually glanced over to Sapphee next to him.

She had the same serious expression she always wore, but her arms were crossed over her chest, and she was gripping her shoulders in her hands. Glenn imagined that the chill winds that blew into the village from the mountaintops were difficult to handle for someone weak to the cold like her. If their clinic building was also made out of wood, Glenn imagined their temporary abode was going to be much cooler than it was back in Lindworm.

Glenn took off his white coat and, without a word, draped it over Sapphee's shoulders.

"Doctor?"

"It's fine, just wear it."

Sapphee didn't say anything back to Glenn, but with a slight smile, she took hold of the coat.

"Now then, we are going to go get a look at Kay's injuries," Glenn said. "What about you, Miss Tisalia?"

"I have something I need to discuss with the village elder—it's regarding a business deal of ours." Her words implied that the conversation would be a private one for just the two of them and she gave a wink to the village elder. Glenn watched the deep nod that the village elder gave Tisalia in return and thought to himself that there must have been some sort of previous negotiation between the two of them.

"Lorna," Tisalia said, "go with the doctor. I'm worried about Kay, too."

"Understood, Mistress."

Glenn was reassured to have her with them. Without saying a word, Lorna started walking out in front as though she were Glenn's guide. Judging from her movements, Glenn suspected that Lorna had also been to the village on a number of previous occasions.

The dwellings built into the bluffs were the harpies' places of residence. As such, the residences built at the base of the ravine were for children, the elderly, or harpies who were too sick to fly. Buildings for guests could also be found there, prepared for visiting species that had no wings of their own.

They were still following Lorna's lead when the dwelling the harpies had prepared for them finally came into view. The carriage Glenn and Sapphee had ridden in was stopped nearby. The building they were to stay in was made out of wood, but its round and sturdy-looking pillars and grass-thatched roof made it look like it had been conscientiously created. It was a splendid building, one that wouldn't compare unfavorably with houses made of stone.

"Excuse me," Glenn said and entered the house.

Already, the fairies they had brought with them from their clinic were organizing their equipment and running around the inside of the house. Glenn was grateful that he could leave the miscellaneous tasks like cleaning up the examination tools and equipment to the hardworking helper fairies. It meant that he could devote all of his efforts to examining and treating patients.

The building was spacious, with a bedroom and a simple kitchen. It didn't seem like they would have a difficult time living there. In addition, there had been a number of beds prepared for the patients. The space left nothing to be desired.

It was a grave situation that there wasn't a doctor in the village. They had all the necessary equipment, as well as buildings like the one he was now in, but had no one who could diagnose and treat harpies.

"This could be quite a nice place for us to live, Dr. Glenn," Sapphee said. "The two of us could stay here quietly, and without Dr. Cthulhy around to interfere..."

"We have patients waiting for us back in Lindworm. You know we can't do that."

"I know." Sapphee pouted her lips and sulked.

The clinic back in Lindworm currently had a sign on the door saying they weren't seeing any patients while they were gone. It informed his regular patients that while Glenn was away on his trip to the harpy village, they should visit the Lindworm Central Hospital. The director there was Glenn's teacher, Cthulhy, and he felt it was fine to leave his patients in her care while he was gone.

Kay was sleeping in one of the rooms prepared for the patients admitted into Glenn's makeshift clinic. But she wasn't sleeping on the bed. It appeared it had been too small for her large build, so she was lying on her side on some straw that had been spread out over the floor. She woke when they came in.

"How are you feeling, Kay?" Lorna asked. With her companion injured, she had accompanied Glenn and Sapphee with a blank, unchanging expression.

"I just twisted it. You don't need to worry."

"I don't think so," Glenn said. "When you consider a centaur's weight, falling down can put a significant amount of strain on the body, and it's very likely that bones may be broken. It's not something to take lightly."

"Doctor, honestly, you're exaggerating... Ow!" Kay gave a big smile but appeared to still have some pain as her expression quickly changed into a grimace.

Given her condition, Glenn was beginning to think that his trip away from the clinic might have to last even longer. With her legs like this, Kay wouldn't be able to go down the mountain, and they couldn't just leave her behind in the village. It was only the beginning, but it seemed that Glenn's visit already had many difficulties lying ahead.

"Well, then," Sapphee said, "it seems we'll be starting work immediately. Doesn't it, Dr. Glenn?"

"Indeed, it does."

Glenn gently touched Kay's legs. He had been right after all. He felt heat around her fetlock—the joint between her knee and her hoof. It appeared that area was the one affected.

"Now, then—I will begin my examination."

✗ ✗ ✗ ✗ ✗

There was nothing unusual about Kay's bones. Glenn could sense heat and see swelling at her fetlock joint, and Kay herself seemed to be in pain, but she had no difficulty in moving it. Glenn thought there wasn't any reason to worry about her having a broken bone.

"I'm going to move your leg a little."

"Okay... Um, gently please, Doctor."

"Of course."

Glenn slowly started to put strain on her fetlock. Her leg was covered in lustrous chestnut hair, and her coat made one want to pass one's hand over it forever. Glenn had no doubt that she took care to properly brush herself all the way down to the bottom of her legs.

Gradually, Glenn started to bend her leg left and right.

"Augh!"

"Here it is. It does look like a sprain after all. The leg's twisted outwards."

"Unh, ah!"

"It doesn't seem to have any impact on the ligament. It's probably just the joint, isn't it?"

"D-Doctor...! Th-that area... It hurts!"

"Oh, of course, sorry." Stopping at Kay's cries, Glenn took his hands off her in a panic.

Although her leg was sprained, the amount of pain she felt

was still excessive. Glenn thought that it must have gotten quite severely twisted. The fact she hadn't ended up with any broken bones was a lucky consolation.

Her firm and resolute expression was just the same as always, but Glenn thought she was surely exerting herself quite a bit to look so calm and composed.

"You will definitely need to stay in bed and rest for a sprain this severe."

"I-If there are no bones broken, then I can walk... Ah, ow!"

"See? Right after I told you, too."

After that, Glenn, Sapphee, and Lorna all recommended that Kay get some rest. If she forced herself to walk around, it would only take her longer to fully heal. However, if she stayed in bed, a compress and pain medication would be more than enough to treat the sprain.

Glenn's diagnosis was that she would be fully recovered in half a month.

"Fortunately, it seems the hot springs in the village are currently active," Glenn told Kay, sticking a compress to her front leg and wrapping a bandage around it so she wouldn't put any unnecessary stress on it.

With her legs elevated, Glenn left the limbs as they were. He had lifted up her skirt slightly; if someone were to see them, they would have doubtless misunderstood what was going on—*No, no,* Glenn thought to himself. This was nothing more than an examination. There was nothing wrong with the way he worked.

"If you can take a dip in the hot springs, do so—it should

hasten your recovery. For now, please rest."

Lorna smiled profoundly and said, "While you're gone, Kay, I'll make sure to look after our mistress."

Glenn was sure that Kay was finally able to relax after seeing her partner nod after that statement, filled with confidence and resolve.

"In that case, I'll treat this as an opportunity to take a vacation and take it easy. Make sure you don't fail in your duties, Lorna."

"Of course. Leave it to me, Kay."

Lorna put her hand across her chest and gave a smile full of confidence.

× × × × ×

With this, Kay slept tucked under a layer of straw in a corner of the makeshift clinic.

As their first admitted patient of the trip, Glenn would have liked to properly keep watch over her, but he couldn't just focus his efforts on Kay. There were still many harpies in the village waiting for him to treat them.

An expecting mother almost ready to lay her eggs and looking almost full to bursting. A young harpy that had fallen out of the sky and broken their right arm. An old woman complaining of a pain in her back, and a child who had been stricken with a cold that was going around. In just the first day, the patients came in one right after another.

Glenn was busy enough that he thought his eyes would spring straight out of his head.

"You're quite popular, aren't you, Doctor?" Sapphee jokingly whispered into his ear.

While Glenn had come prepared, he found himself even busier than he had imagined. Dealing with the injured and prescribing medicine to the sick, Glenn managed a large amount of work.

Sapphee was just as busy as Glenn. She had to create various kinds of medicine for the different patients, but she was able to do several jobs at once, writing down the patients' charts with her right hand, selecting the necessary medicinal herbs with her left, and using her tail to handle the mortar and pestle. She hummed along as she completed the various medications.

On top of all that, she was adept at directing and commanding the servant fairies and was many times more efficient than Glenn was at his work. Everything from guiding patients to the examination rooms to handling their final payments was in her realm of control.

Even without the fairies, the fact that just the two of them could manage the clinic themselves was largely because of Sapphee's competency.

Furthermore, rumor was spreading around the village that a doctor had arrived, and that brought guests to the clinic who weren't patients at all.

"Doctor!"

"Oh, it's the doctor! Hello!"

As dusk approached, a group of young harpy girls came to

impose on the clinic.

Glenn recognized them. These were the young harpies who had been taken by the slave traders on the Merrow Waterways. Of all the harpies who had been freed, these girls were the ones without any home to return to, who had been taken in by the village. Back then, they all looked sickly and were trembling in fear, but now the young harpy girls all looked at Glenn with bright, healthy smiles.

Their shrill cries echoed in the clinic. Harpy voices carried for long distances to begin with, but their current cries were even higher than normal.

The feathers on the harpies all had a glossy sheen to them. Completely different from their time in imprisonment, it appeared to Glenn that they were all in perfect health.

"...You're quite popular—huh, Doctor?" With the harpy girls coming in one after another to say hello to Glenn, Sapphee's mood now seemed to be much worse as she spoke to him.

Pacifying the enraged Sapphee, her veins bulging out of her forehead, Glenn finished up the first day of work at their makeshift clinic.

It didn't need saying, but he was exhausted. He felt this was partly due to the fact they had quickly jumped right into their medical work after the long journey without a moment's rest.

Sapphee, however, was not showing any exhaustion from the trip and worked energetically in the clinic. While Glenn knew that he needed to follow her example, he couldn't do anything to get rid of his sense of fatigue.

"It's because it's the first day," Sapphee told Glenn. "At first it might be hectic, but it will slowly calm down. Once it does, we'll be able to take a break."

"It'd be nice if it played out like that..."

With just the first day as an indicator, Glenn could already tell that there were even more patients than he had expected. That said, properly coping with any emergency patients was the very purpose of his job as a doctor. Illness and injury didn't strike only when it was convenient for Glenn.

On top of that, patients always seemed to come just as he was starting to think to himself that things had quieted down a bit. If he weren't prepared for such occurrences, he wouldn't be able to help his monster patients.

Glenn focused his mind again on the work ahead of him.

× × ✖ × ×

A few days had passed since Glenn had arrived in the village.

Just as Sapphee had said, the foot traffic through the clinic had gradually tapered off. With it, Glenn had more opportunities to take a break. However, even with that being the case, Glenn certainly wasn't taking any sort of long and relaxing periods of rest.

Whether he realized it himself or not, Glenn was a workaholic.

When the patients coming to his temporary clinic dropped in number, he thought about how there might be patients who couldn't walk of their own accord. That was just his personality.

As such, Glenn carried his personal medical bag and made visits all over the village, enough to become acclimated to the village itself. Again, this was simply how Glenn was—he had a tendency to work excessively, unable to stop even if someone else tried to make him.

Unable to go outside very easily, Sapphee stayed in the clinic and examined patients. Having a broad and general knowledge of medicine, she had become accustomed to managing the clinic while Glenn was gone. Even there in the village, she (along with the fairies) had immediately been entrusted with looking after the clinic while he was out.

Just like back in the city, Glenn rushed about the village so he could begin to verify that all of the harpies there were properly healthy and not suffering any ailments or injuries. What concerned him was the reason he had come to the village in the first place— the harpy, Illy, whose feathers had fallen out and who was no longer able to fly. Glenn had tried many times to meet with Illy, but it seemed she was despondent and said she didn't want to see Glenn.

She must have been in a considerably terrible condition to not want to see a doctor—or at least, that's what Glenn thought. He had heard that the village elder had tried to persuade her a number of times to show her condition to Glenn, but Illy herself was persistent in saying she didn't want to be seen.

Glenn hoped that he would be able to examine her before long, but until then, he could only run about the village frantically.

Tisalia could be seen frantically pacing about, as well—all over the village. Glenn initially assumed she had some sort of work to do for Scythia Transportation. However, immediately after talking with the village elder and meeting with each of the village's leaders, she would stare up at the harpies' huts on the precipices of the bluff.

Tisalia's passion for her work was similar to Glenn's.

Glenn wasn't worried about Tisalia as she ran about the village—instead, he was concerned about one of her attendants.

"Miss Lorna?" Glenn called out to the centaur, who was standing alone in the village.

"Oh, if it isn't Dr. Glenn..."

"What's the matter? Standing out here alone like this..." As far as Glenn knew, Lorna was never alone.

Usually, she could be found accompanying her mistress Tisalia, working on something with Kay, or together with the both of them. Seeing her standing there by herself, Glenn had felt something was off and called out to her because of it.

"No, I'm not alone. I'm with my mistress."

"I don't see her around..."

"I've just lost sight of her a little, that's all... Honestly, no matter how much my mistress grows up, she still has some childishness left in her." Lorna chuckled. Her behavior was ladylike and graceful. Judging by her mannerisms alone, she seemed perfectly normal. And yet...

In reality, the harpy village was small. Small enough that it was very difficult to think one could get lost there.

Naturally, there were many huts projecting out from the bluffs, with many harpies coming and going through the air.

Even at that very moment, there were harpies flying over Glenn's head. They glided from bluff to bluff. Glenn could almost hear them cutting through the wind. Indeed, the village was full of life. However, this was only true of the area where the harpies flew in between the two bluffs. On the ground, things were a bit more quiet. There were at most twenty dwellings at the bottom of the ravine for those who were unable to fly. The space between the two bluffs certainly wasn't large enough for one to get lost in.

All in all, it made Glenn wonder just how likely it was that Lorna could "lose sight" of her mistress here, when she was always hovering closely behind Tisalia.

"How is Kay doing?" Lorna asked, ignoring Glenn's puzzlement.

"Uh... Well, there haven't been any problems in particular. She's sleeping in the temporary clinic, reading books, and the like. Sapphee's been bringing her to the hot springs, and they seem to be having a curative effect on her."

Kay was being an obedient and proper patient.

Well, not exactly, Glenn thought. Occasionally, she would complain that she wanted to practice with her sword, or other warrior-like sentiments, but these were few and far between. It seemed that Kay understood well enough that taking it easy and getting lots of rest was the best way for her injuries to heal.

"This might be a rude question to ask, but—" Glenn thought this was a good opportunity and decided to ask Lorna something that had been on his mind for a while.

"What is the relationship between you and Kay? You're not...
sisters, right?"

"Are you curious? Oh, Doctor, come now."

Lorna gave a suggestive smile. The bewitching look wasn't
something one would see when she was beside the lively, vigorous Kay.

"We're war orphans."

"Orphans...?"

"That's right. Since centaurs have a long history of working
as mercenaries, it is our custom to take in children who've lost
their parents. The orphans aren't just taken in as normal children,
though—they are raised as attendants and soldiers. People may
call us warmongers, but it's one reason we have continued to exist
to this day."

It was a world Glenn knew nothing about, but the rule among
the centaurs was to esteem death on the battlefield. There were
naturally many who died in battle, and for this reason, it wasn't
at all strange for there to be children who had lost their parents.
Glenn thought it was probably inevitable that a culture developed where orphans were raised by a specific family.

In other words, the children without parents were raised together by everyone. However, Glenn wondered why the children
were then taken in as attendants. Then it occurred to him that
this might have been to avoid entangling the orphans in disputes
of succession and inheritance.

"Since we were taken in as orphans by a prestigious family
like the Scythia, serving our mistress is the purpose of both my

life and Kay's."

Lorna showed no hesitation in her eyes. Glenn felt a sharpness in them, like an arrow flying straight and true through the air. He thought he caught a glimpse of something sinister and ominous in the gaze of the bodyguard maid.

"We were personally raised by the current steward of the Scythia Company. He was our adoptive father, and Kay and I took his last name. My full name is Lorna Arte."

"Is that so?"

"Since she was taken in before, Kay Arte became my older sister, but...I've never really thought of her as an older sister. She has a bit of a mischievous streak in her, after all."

Lorna with her well-bred, somewhat mysterious air. Kay with her plain, somewhat prophetic and philosophical awareness. The two struck a good balance, and Glenn imagined that this was precisely why Tisalia had put her trust in both of them and why the two of them cared so deeply for their mistress.

And now...

Kay was not at Lorna's side. Glenn wondered if the accident had caused their harmonious balance to come undone. Lorna's tone of voice was absolutely unchanged from her normal way of speaking, but there was still some part of it that made Glenn feel like she was restless.

"Lorna!"

The sound of hooves came from behind Glenn.

Tisalia was rushing over to where he and Lorna stood.

"Lorna! What are you doing over here?! Oh hello, Dr. Glenn."

"I was just asking the doctor about Kay's condition," Lorna said. "But I should be asking you, Mistress: How did you end up getting lost?"

"You're the one who's gone and gotten herself lost! The moment I take my eyes off you, you go wandering off in a daze!"

"...Huh?" Lorna quirked her head at Tisalia's scolding, as if she had no idea what she was talking about.

Tisalia put her head in her hands, unsure what she should do. Lorna didn't seem to understand why her mistress was acting this way, instead looking even more vacant and absentminded than before.

Glenn thought to himself—*could this situation be even graver than I imagined?*

× × ✖ × ×

"Lorna is acting strange! Very strange!"

That night, Tisalia visited Glenn and Sapphee's borrowed hut.

"Honestly!" she shouted. "How did it get this way?! What could have happened...?"

Munch.

"How about you choose between angrily ranting or eating your food?" Sapphee said calmly.

"I'm *not* angry!" Tisalia rebutted. She didn't appear to be mad, per se, but rather seemed unsure about what she should use as an outlet for her emotions.

Glenn stared at Tisalia with a troubled look on his face.

She had timed her visit to arrive just as they were switching the sign on the clinic to closed for the day. Before Glenn could ask her what her business was, a loud growling had come up from her stomach, so he had proposed they all eat something for the time being and indeed...it appeared that she had been *quite* hungry. She had engrossed herself in gulping down the salad Sapphee prepared for the horsewoman princess.

Centaurs were heavy eaters.

Nevertheless, they were vegetarians, and didn't consume anything besides vegetables and greens. However, vegetables were an inefficient source of the nutrients necessary to support centaurs' active bodies and high metabolism. As a result, they ate huge amounts of food at once. Even at the large Alraune Plantation, the customers were primarily centaurs. There were some other vegetarian races of monster, but in general, the centaurs were the most voracious eaters.

Tisalia easily devoured a large plate overflowing with salad. It had nothing but dressing on it for seasoning. For omnivores like lamia and humans, it was a very difficult diet to understand.

"Absolutely delicious. You're pretty good at cooking, Miss Sapphee."

"That's just because I make Dr. Glenn's meals for him every day. If the doctor is left on his own, he's quick to start skimping out on his food." Sapphee thrust out her chest in pride, but even Glenn would have been able to cut up the vegetables needed to make something as simple as a salad. He didn't feel like it was anything for her to act so superior over.

"Hmph," he said. "Perhaps I should start studying how to cook..."

"More importantly..." Sapphee turned her sharp gaze to Tisalia, looking annoyed. "What business did you have with us? I'm sure you didn't just come here for dinner, correct?"

"Oh no, you're right. I came here to intrude on you for dinner." The honest Tisalia held out her plate as though she were asking for seconds. Glenn didn't overlook the twitch in Sapphee's eyebrows that appeared with Tisalia's words. "That's because, you see...lately, my meals have been strange."

Sapphee was silent, but Tisalia still went ahead and took a heaping portion of salad for herself and began eating again. It was true after all—a centaur's appetite was *far* beyond normal.

"What's been strange about them?" Sapphee asked.

"Lorna is making them for me, but...she uses the wrong seasonings, and while I'm eating, she seems to have her head in the clouds. To top it all off, she cut herself with her knife. She's been practically the definition of clumsiness."

"Is that...really true?" Glenn couldn't imagine the Lorna he knew acting in such a way.

Then again, when he thought back to earlier that day, perhaps it wasn't as hard to believe as he had first thought. In the harpy village, which was far too small for anyone to get lost in, Lorna had been standing absentmindedly by herself. After seeing how Tisalia scolded her after the fact, Lorna was clearly the one who had been lost.

After completely devouring the second plate of salad, Tisalia wiped the corners of her mouth with a handkerchief.

"Absolutely true! I haven't had a single proper meal since we've gotten here! Miss Sapphee's cooking, though, is delicious... Truly splendid!" Her reply was so spirited that it seemed she might burst into tears of gratitude.

"I only put dressing on some raw vegetables..." Despite saying this, it seemed that Sapphee wasn't at all displeased with the repeat praise for her cooking, and her tail swayed slowly side to side. It was proof of her good mood. As shown in her reaction, she had an unexpected side to her that made her prickliness easy to deal with. Praising her for her housework was a prime example of this.

Tisalia stiffened her expression and turned to Glenn. "Anyway, it's obvious that there is something weird going on with Lorna! At this rate, I won't be able to eat for the rest of the trip!"

"Well, I don't know about that..."

"On top of it all, she even makes mistakes when changing my clothes! And she kept making irrelevant, off-topic comments during my business meeting with the village elder. Our work isn't moving forward whatsoever! What in the world could be happening to Lorna, I wonder?"

"Business meetings?" Glenn said. "Now that you mention it, what were you discussing with the village elder?"

Tisalia threw out her chest as if she had been eagerly expecting Glenn's question. Her hefty breasts swayed ostentatiously.

"Yes, our business negotiations. This is my very reason for coming all the way here. Within Scythia Transportation, there's been talk of partnering with the harpies and establishing an air transportation branch of the company."

"Air transportation?"

"By hiring the harpies with their splendid flight ability, we can create a service specializing in express delivery and messenger services. With such an addition, we can expect to have even greater profits."

"I see..."

Glenn couldn't help but be impressed. It certainly sounded like a good idea to him.

By pulling carts, the centaurs were able to transport humans and large loads of cargo. However, they couldn't adapt at all to new circumstances. When they were tasked to quickly deliver a small package, it was inefficient for them to dedicate a whole carriage to one item.

That's where the harpies came in. Flying in the air, free from the restrictions that came with road travel, they could readily deliver packages in a short amount of time. While flying through the air meant carrying heavy packages would be difficult, they would be prompt at delivering letters and small parcels.

Glenn immediately thought to himself about how this might affect his own clinic.

For example, he could promptly receive notice of a patient in need of emergency care and rush out to the scene far quicker than usual. Also, if the harpies delivered letters, he could send diagnoses to places like the harpy village where there was no doctor and would be able to just send the necessary medicine as needed. That kind of service would be quite beneficial for him when treating patients.

"An air transport service specializing in speed and affordability," Tisalia continued. "To make it happen, we're speaking with the village elder and currently negotiating whether or not we would be able to hire harpies that want to work for our company."

"I see. I think that's a great idea."

"From the beginning, Scythia Transportation has been a single-species operation, and there are many voices within the company who oppose employing non-centaurs, but...I've come to quiet that dissent. I believe if we can get results on this trip, the opposition group within the company will grow silent and agree to the idea."

With these internal affairs swirling about, the representative and only daughter of the company's owner had deliberately come to the village and moved forward with negotiations. Glenn thought that, since this was the case, Scythia Transportation must be quite serious about the idea. Tisalia was already involved in even the rather detailed, deep parts of managing the company.

He could now see the sense of responsibility and the heavy pressure that was weighing on Tisalia's shoulders.

"They're very important business negotiations!" Tisalia said. "And yet, Kay is injured, and Lorna has become so strange! Doctor, can you look at Lorna, as well?!"

"You mean...examine her medically?" Glenn asked. Kay's sprain was naturally within his specialization. Lorna's condition, however, was neither an illness nor an injury. Glenn believed it to be something psychological. "Miss Lorna is probably so distracted because her partner Miss Kay isn't with her... Or rather, she's worried about Miss Kay's injuries... Right?"

Tisalia nodded. "In all likelihood, that's what I think the problem is."

"In which case, there's nothing you can really do but wait until Miss Kay's sprain is healed..."

Sprains tended to be regarded lightly but could be a surprisingly troublesome injury to have. Whether human or monster, a patient's sense of their own body was less correct than one might have thought. With the pain of the sprain gone, one might think they were better and could return to living the same way they had before their sprain. That was not the case, however, as there was the possibility that they might lose feeling in their previously injured limb and fall—causing yet another sprain to occur.

It was a doctor's job to closely monitor the progression of the sprain and determine when it was completely healed. The worst that could happen was for someone uneducated on the subject to decide the injury had healed when in truth it hadn't.

"In that case, I've truly lost it all!" Tisalia said. "I can't bear to have both Kay and Lorna not doing their jobs!"

"You can manage without any attendants, can't you?" Glenn asked.

"Absolutely out of the question! It's impossible for me to live without my attendants! Up until now, Lorna and Kay have even helped me tie my hair and change my clothes!"

"Do it yourself," Sapphee stated flatly, in response to Tisalia's spoiled remarks.

Sapphee wasn't simply being cold to Tisalia. There were just some things that they couldn't do as doctors. What aid could they give to a vacant, absentminded centaur who was worried about her companion? At most, they could talk to her about it and do their best to watch out for her.

On the other hand, Glenn thought, there was no way to quickly heal Kay's sprain. It was best for her to soak herself in the hot springs when able and to stay in bed—which was exactly what Kay was doing.

"In that case," Tisalia said, "I guess I have no other choice." With a thump, she placed something on top of the table. It was a bottle.

A label was glued onto the bottle, marked with a crest that depicted a large, blooming rose. Glenn recognized the crest and wondered where Tisalia had even been hiding the bottle in the first place.

"How is this, then?! It's from my company's reserve! The highest quality white wine, made with the grapes of the Alraune Plantation! It's a special vintage—only ten bottles are produced a year! I'm offering it to you!"

"We will absolutely help. No, please—*let us* help," Sapphee answered immediately, her eyes dazzled by the lure of alcohol.

"Hold on a second, Sapphee..." Glenn said.

"It's an Alraune white wine! This chance may only come once in a lifetime! You can't let this opportunity pass you by!" Tisalia said. She appeared to be weak but was quite determined. Glenn thought that she must have deliberately brought the bottle as a secret plan to ask for Sapphee's help. As was to be expected of the sole heiress representing her company, she seemed to have gotten the better of Sapphee in her negotiations.

However, Glenn was still calm and collected.

Whether they were given expensive wine or not didn't change the fact that there wasn't anything they could do to treat Lorna. However, it didn't seem that Sapphee was going to be convinced, having already taken the bottle of wine and coiled her tail around it so no one would take it from her.

"Doctor." Tisalia seemed to have realized that Glenn was still hesitating. Her gaze was aimed directly ahead and pierced through Glenn. "You might have heard already, but Kay and Lorna were originally orphans."

"Oh, yeah. A little bit, a while back." Glenn evaded the question without mentioning it was something he had just happened to ask about earlier that afternoon. He thought that if he told Tisalia he had broached such a serious topic in passing small talk, she would only take offense.

"The three of us were raised almost like sisters, ever since we were little. But in the end, I'm still their lady, and they are my attendants. There are surely things that they can't share with me but that they share in common between themselves. There are some things I cannot join them in." Tisalia's words had a tinge of loneliness to them.

In truth, Tisalia wanted to connect with them like sisters and as friends.

However, she would forever be unable to have such a comfortable relationship. For Tisalia, her lineage and social status were her source of pride. Even without being told, keeping one's status in mind was something that was imposed on her. Considering how she had looked earlier in the day, Lorna and Kay also had a line they didn't cross with their mistress.

"It's an old centaur custom," Tisalia explained, "but it's said that on long-distance marches, there were many people who would get injured and become unable to run. Speed is paramount for a centaur soldier; they have to move as quickly as possible. But if you become injured and can't do that... Well, at times like that, low-status soldiers are then forced to commit suicide. Those with status could also be forced to end their own life—but with their mistresses helping by beheading them. That's how it used to be."

"Centaurs did things like that...? But why?"

"Being captured by the enemy was shameful. And slowing the march because of your own injury was also shameful. It's a bad tradition born entirely out of the centaur's proud nature. There are many stories left behind of splendid officers and soldiers being lost and defeated in battles because of that sort of pride." Tisalia laughed and added, "That's why nowadays, it's a custom that's long been done away with."

Glenn understood what Tisalia was saying—if it had been a different time, Kay might have ended up beheaded by Tisalia's own hands. Glenn couldn't even imagine the feeling of being killed by the master one had sworn their loyalty to, nor could he imagine the other side of the situation—killing the subordinates who had placed their trust in you.

"We're in an age of peace now, and that's why it's something that's no longer necessary. But Lorna knows this custom very well, and that's why she's lost her head so much after Kay's injury."

Nothing more than a sprain—but that wasn't entirely true.

In a different time, it would have been a severe injury that dictated one's life or death. At the very least, that's how it would have been for a centaur.

"I'm begging you, Doctor. Please do something." Both Tisalia's gaze and her words were honest and straightforward.

Her earnest request was one that would have moved just about anyone, but Glenn was touched, for the centaur's words had no ulterior motives—or anything of the sort—in them. Glenn even thought that by being this straightforward, it actually seemed like *she* was the one being tricked and taken in.

"...Okay. I'll accept."

"Really?"

"Yes... In the end, I can't bear to let her stay as she is, either. Are you listening, Sapphee?" Glenn addressed his assistant as she was merrily putting away the expensive wine.

She didn't look up as she replied. "I'm listening. It sounds tough, but I hope you'll do your best, Doctor."

With her being taken in by the wine, Glenn wanted to make sure *she* was going to do her best.

Tisalia looked between Glenn and Sapphee for a few moments, and then finally stood up with a deep bow. "I'm putting all of my trust in both of you."

✖ ✖ ✖ ✖ ✖

Glenn had accepted the task.

However, that didn't mean he had any sort of bright ideas. There was nothing else he could do about the situation, so in the meantime, he pored over every medical book relating to centaurs that he had brought with him from the clinic. In the next few days that followed, whenever he had down time between examinations, he would chase after the complicated words and charts in the books.

"We didn't really bring many medical books with us, did we, huh...?"

They had brought the books they *did* have with them as a precaution, in case they came across a case they didn't have much experience with. However, they hadn't been able to pack very many books into the carriage, as taking too many would have caused trouble for Tisalia when she pulled the cart.

On the other hand, when he thought about whether he'd find a good solution even if he did return to Lindworm, Tisalia's request remained a difficult one.

"It'd be nice if I could ask Dr. Cthulhy for advice..." His former teacher, Cthulhy Squele, came to mind.

She was a female scylla, an aquatic species of monster. With her impressive intellectual looks and lower body made up of eight tentacles, she could generally handle anything that came her way. Glenn believed his teacher would have been able to deal with

Lorna's current poor condition immediately.

He shook his head and told himself he couldn't think that way.

If he relied on his teacher after becoming independent, it would mean he was acknowledging his lack of personal growth as a doctor. There was no way someone as strict as Cthulhy would forgive him for being so inexperienced.

Cthulhy had been the one to order him to come up to the harpy village in the first place. What was the point of him coming here if he couldn't solve the difficult problems he was being confronted with?

"Does it seem like there's a way to work things out, Doctor?" Sapphee asked, appearing with a basket full of fruit hanging from her tail. The harpies of the village offered the two of them fruits, meats, nuts, and wild mountain vegetables, as well. Whether it was as a thank-you for their services, or they were simply just sharing their food, it seemed that Sapphee had received another gift.

"Nope, not at all."

"Is it that difficult a problem?"

"It's not really difficult... Miss Lorna's absentminded and out of it because of Miss Kay's injury. Since she is worried about Miss Kay's sprain, she has become neglectful of a variety of her duties... But knowing all that doesn't make a difference."

The problem was that Glenn couldn't get rid of the cause of her problems.

It would still take some time to treat Kay's sprain—and on

top of that, there were some things that only natural self-recovery could take care of.

"I wonder if, with some pain medicine and a splint...if Kay could walk," Glenn said. "Even still, she would heal quicker if she just rested in the clinic."

"I would think that seeing Miss Kay with a splint on her leg would only serve to worry Miss Lorna even further," Sapphee replied.

"That's a good point, too..."

As far as Kay's treatment was concerned, it was best to have her stay bedridden in the clinic as she had been since they had arrived.

"Instead," Sapphee said, "what about having Miss Lorna stay by Miss Kay's side and look after her until she's healed?"

"If we do that, then that would mean Miss Tisalia wouldn't have anyone to attend to her."

"She's already a well-grown adult—she'll only have more problems if she doesn't learn to become a little self-sufficient. Can she really do nothing on her own without her attendants?"

"I think she is an incredible person, but she's still a daughter of a wealthy, influential family... She'll probably come again to have dinner here, you know?"

Sapphee's face showed that she was clearly not a fan of the idea. It appeared that being forced to act like Tisalia's waiter was something that rubbed her the wrong way. Glenn thought that Sapphee was more suited to being the owner of a high-end lounge than being a waitress at some small-town watering hole.

He imagined Sapphee waving a cocktail shaker with her tail and came close to bursting out laughing.

"Miss Lorna seemed to be calm when I saw her, though," Glenn said.

"If she herself isn't aware of it, it must be a serious case. That said, Miss Kay is composed and calm even when acting separately from Miss Lorna."

"I suppose it's a difference in their personalities." Even if they had a similar air about them, they were still separate individuals, after all.

Glenn continued to ponder over the situation. Lorna wasn't sick. If she had some sort of mental depression, then her condition would have been in Glenn's territory, but she was suffering from something different. She simply had something on her mind and was distracted by it.

A similar case had been recorded in the medical books Glenn brought with him. The book described the centaurs as courageous and well-versed in martial arts, but it also mentioned that they had nervous and cowardly parts to them as well. Glenn thought that this sensitivity might be one of Lorna's characteristics—and a dominant one.

"Miss Lorna's rather sensitive, isn't she?" Sapphee said.

"Careful with how you say that, Sapphee... Someone could misunderstand."

Sapphee nonchalantly gave an ominous reply: "Smoothing over the fact won't change anything. Besides, Dr. Glenn—if she's sensitive, then that means she needs to be dealt with accordingly."

"Dealt with...?"

"As part of an assassin's arsenal, medicine can dull and suppress pain in certain situations, and the body becomes able to move even through injury." Sapphee slipped her tongue out of her mouth with her smile.

For generations, Sapphee's family had been medicine makers, while also working as assassins in the untold annals of history. There were parts of Sapphee's knowledge of pharmacology that originated from the skills and techniques of assassination. Glenn felt a vague sense of fear looking at Sapphee's smile and her suspicious snake eyes.

However, poison and medicine were two sides of the same coin.

Sapphee was now a splendid pharmacologist. If he didn't have the anesthesia she administered when it was time to perform surgeries, Glenn wouldn't even be able to operate.

Glenn thought to himself that this was a subtle hint on how to solve the problem from his old teacher's senior pupil.

"You don't... You're not actually saying to use drugs, right?"

"There isn't any need to go that far," she said. "If she is concerned about things around her, you just need to close off those surroundings."

Close off those surroundings...

It all made sense to Glenn after hearing those words. A solution to the issue had appeared. He wondered if Sapphee had only pretended to get drawn in by the high-quality wine—perhaps she had her eyes on the proper treatment long ago.

If that were the case, she should have told him sooner, Glenn thought, until he realized something. Sapphee was purposely giving her suggestion in a roundabout way so Glenn would come to the solution himself. It must have been her way of telling him to find the answer on his own—her form of encouragement.

Glenn felt ashamed. Sapphee was nothing more than a pharmacologist. Even if he left the medicine up to her, he was still the only doctor. If he were always turning to his teacher or his teacher's more experienced pupil for help, his position would be meaningless. He was the only one who could properly treat both Kay and Lorna.

In this village without any doctor, he was the only one who could heal those around him.

"But you know, Sapphee, if you had intended to accept Tisalia's request in the first place, just be straightforward about it. It would make Tisalia happier."

"Well, obviously I wanted to drink the wine, too."

Glenn couldn't help but show exasperation at Sapphee's shamelessness.

He wondered when she would open up her treasured bottle. He was sure she wouldn't open it unless it was for an extremely big celebration of some kind.

"Anyway..." he said, flipping through the pages of one of his medical books. "Now, where was it? Here we go." He finally found the page that detailed a centaur's growth through childhood.

"Doctor?" Sapphee looked over his shoulder. "Centaur maturation, education...possible disorders and how to treat them?

Doctor, what exactly are you planning to do? Miss Lorna is already a grown woman."

"Well, of course I know that..."

The book contained detailed commentary, along with the charts and images about a centaur's childhood. Glenn turned the pages even further and read all of the necessary information.

Sapphee tilted her head emphatically. It seemed that even if she understood what was needed to help Lorna, her thought process hadn't extended far enough to know what method they would use to actually administer her treatment.

This was exactly why it couldn't be done without Glenn.

As a doctor, Glenn had to be able to do what was asked of him. He needed to be able to treat the patient in the most appropriate way possible in response to the proposal Sapphee had given him.

"Sapphee, can you ask the fairies to deliver a message?"

"What? Oh, y-yes. To whom?"

"To Miss Tisalia. I want to ask her if she has any of these tools with her."

Glenn pointed to the picture in the corner of the page.

Looking at where he was pointing, doubt and quandary began to fill Sapphee's snake eyes.

✷ ✖ ✖ ✖ ✷

Lorna Arte had always had Kay Arte by her side.

The period of Lorna's life when she didn't have her stepsister at her side reminded her of her cruel time as an orphan. Children who lost their parents in a time of war faced suffering that was impossible to try and explain with a single word or sentence.

For Lorna, having Kay with her was proof that she was an employee of the company, her own confirmation of her place where she belonged, and it had the same meaning to her as serving Tisalia did.

Compared to Kay, Lorna had a nervousness and high-strung streak to her. Her personality was one where she would pay attention to many things at once and meddle in this and that. Having such a temperament actually made her well-suited to be Tisalia's handmaiden, but because of that, she was constantly worrying about one thing or another.

Right now, she was worried about the future of the company.

Eventually, Tisalia would lead Scythia Transportation. In order to do so, Tisalia needed to be married immediately and give birth to an heir.

However, Lorna had no intention of handing Tisalia over to some man from who knew where. She wanted Tisalia to be happy. The future of the company was important, but Tisalia's feelings needed to be duly considered as well.

Currently, the object of Tisalia's affection was Dr. Glenn Litbeit, and Lorna honestly thought that he would be a suitable suitor for her. He was a fitting man to take on the responsibilities of the company with Tisalia. Of course, this was all independent of Glenn's feelings on the matter.

And yet...

Kay was injured. Lorna was surprised at how useless she had

become because of Kay's injury. She was unable to handle her chores or her responsibilities as a bodyguard. She was even absentminded when it came to making the sweets she was usually so good at fashioning. Lorna was more of one heart and body with Kay than she had thought. She had always forced that way of being on herself.

But what made her upset was that it seemed this wasn't the case with Kay.

While she may have regretted the sprain she suffered, Kay was leisurely recuperating in a corner of the clinic. Lorna knew that this was what recovery was supposed to be like, but seeing Kay blithely ignoring her concerns as she read books and napped made her just as worried.

She thought to herself, *Is my partner really fine with all of this?*

Even though Lorna had to be so unwavering and resolute herself?

Lorna would unconsciously stop as she walked, her mind vacantly turning to nothing but Tisalia, as her troubles and concerns grew worse and worse.

However—

"Phew..."

The world went dark. Lorna took a deep breath at the fading brightness of her view.

The darkness wasn't unwelcome. If anything, it made her calm. If she had some herbal tea to go with it, she thought that her mood might relax even further. Her thoughts wouldn't bother her and if anything, it would begin to clear her head. She wondered to herself what she had even been worrying about.

"How are you feeling, Miss Lorna?" It was Dr. Glenn's voice.

Lorna couldn't see him, but she knew that he was close by. Her centaur ears, situated on top of her head, could easily determine where a noise was coming from.

"Can you see in front of you?" he asked.

"Yes, Doctor." Lorna nodded, straining her eyes.

The calming darkness that washed over her was due to a very thin black piece of cloth. It wasn't total darkness; she could see through the small loose openings in the cloth's texture. Even with that being the case, it didn't change the fact that her eyes were hidden and her field of vision was greatly restricted.

But to Lorna, it was fine. "It's fantastic...quite fantastic."

There were too many things in the world bothering her. Her hands were small, only able to do housework and hold a bow. Her attempts to do anything and everything were clearly more than she could handle.

There was only one thing that she was able to do.

What could she do for Tisalia?

What could she give to her?

"...Lorna?" Tisalia said. "Are you okay?"

Lorna could see Tisalia's face looking at her through the black cloth. She wore an anxious expression, and it was clear that while Lorna was nothing more than her servant, Tisalia still thought of her as family.

Lorna couldn't express just how grateful Tisalia's expression made her feel. An unconscious smile appeared on her face.

Now she understood. The explanation was simple: she served Tisalia to keep her smiling and laughing, filled to the brim with confidence and pride. With her eyes covered, Lorna finally remembered what it was that she could do.

For a worrier like herself, she thought that covering her eyes was the perfect solution.

✗ ✗ ✗ ✗ ✗

In the range of horse riding equipment, there were masks as well as blinders to conceal the horse's eyes. They covered their heads and were used by parade horses and warhorses alike. While such equipment was ostensibly used for protection and decoration, it was also used to narrow the horse's field of vision.

Horses were said to be one of the more delicate members of the animal kingdom. With their three-hundred-and-sixty-degree range of sight, they became shocked or surprised when something unknown came into view. By narrowing their vision, they became aware of only what was directly in front of them. The equipment for achieving this was known as blinkers—or, as already stated, blinders.

Glenn was now trying to take Lorna's exact measurements.

"Hn... Hgngh!"

Inside the clinic, he had placed a blindfold on her as she sat in front of him. It was made of a thin, black cloth that she could see through to observe what was in front of her. It narrowed her vision and prevented unnecessary things from coming into her view.

In addition to that—

"Ngh... Hn."

Glenn was forcing Lorna to bite down on a belt-shaped bit fastened around her thin lips. The bit didn't completely cover her mouth. It was a thin strap, so she experienced very little pain.

Moreover, the straps reached from her neck down her body, where they passed between her breasts and were fixed in various places with metallic rings. It almost looked like a slaver's restraints, but even with all of the straps running across her body, she didn't put up any sort of resistance at all.

Since the bit was made from a thin strap, it didn't prevent her from being able to talk.

"Hahn... Hn, ah!"

"S-sorry, did it feel a little ticklish?"

"N-not at all, Doctor... I'm okay. You could even make the straps tighter..."

"It might hurt if I tighten them any further."

"I don't mind. No, actually...that might be better..."

The straps ran all over her body, but her arms and legs weren't restrained at all. They coiled out from around the waist of the centaur's upper body.

The blindfold and the gag were all things that Tisalia had had with her. It seemed that they were originally used to punish children and attendants during their education. It was certainly true that having one's whole body restrained with belts and straps would be a suitable form of humiliation, but—

"Nh!"

"I'm sorry, but could you straighten out your back for me... Yes, just like that. That's right, that's good."

"Nhyah! Nhghn! That's good!"

Lorna's body began to react as Glenn fitted the straps across her back. Glenn thought that it would hurt her a little bit, but as he finished, she straightened out her back and had a well-proportioned-looking stature to her.

Mounting everything on her had been no easy feat.

However, the voice that escaped Lorna wasn't one of agony or anything of the sort. As the one treating her, Glenn was relieved it wasn't tough to endure, but...he wondered if Lorna's enjoyment of the treatment wasn't just his imagination.

"Ahn! Yes, Doctor, right there...!" She was reacting as though she was getting a massage, but Glenn knew it shouldn't be anything so simple as that. It was restraining equipment after all. "Aaaahh... That's good...that feels good..."

The restraints weren't just for handing out punishments. According to Glenn's medical books, the straps corrected any deformities in the body's bones and were used to support good posture. Therefore, by using them properly while one is still a child, a centaur can grow up with a properly formed body.

"Ah! Hynaaaaah!"

Glenn didn't know who had made the restraints he had put on Lorna but wondered if it had been someone well versed in centaur osteopathy. That they could be used on either children or adults by adjusting the length was an excellent feature.

It was a little surprising to Glenn that Tisalia had this equipment and had brought it with them to the village.

"...Child..." Tisalia said.

"Huh?"

"When I was a child...if I did something naughty, my mom would put these on me and scold me. She tells me even now to bring them with me...even though there's no way I would use them. Well, I guess I did—on Lorna..." Tisalia mumbled to herself with her eyes cast down. For Tisalia, it was most likely not a story from the past she liked to bring up. It seemed that they weren't to use on Kay and Lorna; instead, they appeared to be Tisalia's own personal belongings.

In any event, to Glenn, there was no mistaking the fact that the belts would play a role in restraining Lorna's hypersensitive heart and mind.

Finally, Glenn just about finished putting on the straps. Lorna struck a beautiful figure with her upper body sticking straight up in front of him, blindfolded and gagged, and the straps running across her body...

"How does it feel, Lorna?" Tisalia asked, worried.

At her question, however, Lorna replied by saying, "It's great... I feel very relaxed. I don't have to think about anything unnecessary, or really anything at all."

"I-Is that so?"

"Yes. My vision is narrow, and my chest is tightened...and you are the only thing I can see, Mistress." Lorna giggled modestly. It was very hard to believe she was being restrained by the way she was acting.

Even through the thin cloth blindfold, she seemed to be looking squarely at Tisalia.

"It's outstandingly effective, then," Tisalia said. "It was so painful for me when I was forced to wear this, though..."

"Th-this is just a guess, but...a lot of it is probably due to Miss Lorna's individual character and tastes...I think." Glenn said.

Taking care not to put too much burden on Lorna's body, Glenn began putting the remaining belts and straps on her, but... judging from the centaur's reactions, he felt that the more stress he put on her body, the happier she was.

"So being tied up makes her happy?" Tisalia asked, puzzled.

"I-I don't exactly think that's it, but... Um, it's hard to explain, huh..." Glenn thought perhaps he was simply under the illusion she liked it. Lorna certainly *seemed* like she was enjoying it all, but that didn't necessarily mean she actually liked being tied up.

Even he only ever felt pain when Sapphee coiled around him. *No, wait*, he thought. Sapphee was brilliant at applying pressure, so he was sure it hadn't just been pain. The indescribable feeling of her cold scales gently wrapping around him was—*No, no, no*, he thought. When Sapphee really wrapped herself around him, there were times he seriously thought his life was in danger, but—

Glenn's thoughts were beginning to head in a strange direction.

He tried as much as possible not to let his inner turmoil show on his face and finished fitting the restraints on Lorna.

"I'm sorry for asking you to do all of this, Doctor." Tisalia bowed her head. "But Lorna already seems to be doing better. You are truly reliable, Dr. Glenn... I'm grateful for all of your help."

"Not at all. There are some things on our end that we'd like to apologize for, as well." Glenn glanced over at Sapphee in the corner of the clinic. She was concentrating on making a dose of medicine with the help of the fairies. Since she had received the wine, she couldn't do anything but take responsibility and see things through to the end.

"Hey, Lorna," Tisalia said.

"Yes, Mistress?"

Tisalia smiled, taking hold of Lorna's hand. With Tisalia's forehead almost touching hers, Lorna should have been able to see her face through her blindfold.

"You consulted with Dr. Glenn before about my hoof problem, right?"

"That's right. We asked him for help."

"You know, that made me so very happy... Well, getting horseshoes is still somewhat scary to me, but..."

It *was* rather like Tisalia that there were still parts of her that disliked being shoed.

"I was happy that you and Kay were thinking about me and worried about me."

"Of course, Mistress. Your happiness is our happiness."

"About that." Embracing Lorna, Tisalia whispered in her ear. "I'm the same way, you know. I love the both of you, too, and I want both of you to always be happy."

"Mistress..." Lorna's voice was shaken. Glenn couldn't tell

through the blindfold, but she might have actually been moved to tears. Glenn was on the verge of crying himself at the emotional display of love between servant and master when—

He glanced toward Sapphee.

She had interrupted her work of grinding herbs in her mortar and stared at the two centaurs with an indescribable look on her face.

"Sapphee?" Glenn said. "Something wrong?"

"No, just... I was curious, but Miss Lorna's going to stay like that for a while, right?"

"Oh, yes, that's what the treatment requires..." Since the problem was with Lorna's mood, she would stay restrained until she had properly relaxed her mind and calmed down.

"If that's the case, then Miss Tisalia... She's going to take Miss Lorna around like that, correct? Going around the harpy village, and negotiating with the village elder?"

"Oh."

Glenn hadn't thought that far ahead.

Glancing over to Tisalia, he saw that her eyes were also opened wide in surprise, suggesting that it had been a blind spot for her, as well. However, Lorna put even more strength into her embrace of Tisalia, as if she had no intention of letting go.

"I will accompany you anywhere, Mistress," she declared, her strong sense of loyalty beating in her chest.

Lorna's recovery went smoothly.

She was always at Tisalia's side, just as she had been before they came up the mountain. She no longer stared off vacantly by herself, and Tisalia no longer had to come to the clinic to eat her dinner.

Lorna was once again a sharp, capable servant, as was her nature.

Finding a way out of her restlessness, she was able to do her work without any problems. She efficiently handled all the tasks that needed doing, even in Kay's absence, and had the energy to do the work of two people all on her own.

Glenn himself hadn't expected such a dramatic result from the treatment.

Well, he thought, *there* is *one slight problem.*

Her appearance.

She was, after all, walking around blindfolded, which made her stick out like a sore thumb. The same was true of Tisalia, who lead her along, and the village elder's face looked rather stiff upon greeting the pair.

Lorna had her maid outfit on, but Glenn knew that underneath it she was tightly bound by belts and straps. Lorna had listened to Tisalia's pleas to at least hide the belts under her clothing and the result was moving. Now, Lorna was more vigorous and lively while she worked and seemed to be feeling even better than normal with the restraints on her.

"Lorna's become quite absurd without me around, hasn't she?" Kay muttered in astonishment.

The same as ever, she was resting in the bed of straw in a

corner of the clinic. Glenn had managed to free up some time and was examining her leg. The swelling had gone down a fair amount, perhaps an effect of her time spent in the hot springs.

As he felt her fetlock area, however, Kay's shoulders trembled with surprise.

"Ngh! Doctor, that area's a little too much..."

"It hurts? Hmm... It seems it will still take some time to heal."

Although her sprain had gotten much better, if she were still in pain, Glenn felt it was better for her to remain bedridden.

"Doctor, can I still not move it at all?"

"Of course. No strenuous exercise. I'd also ask you to stay indoors as much as possible."

"Maybe I could go peek in and see how my mistress is doing—"

"Absolutely not."

"Practice swings with my swords, then?"

"Out of the question."

Glenn couldn't believe what she was asking to do, considering the condition her sprain was in. Kay gave a long sigh at Glenn's sharp answers. Both she and Lorna both had a gentle, modest air about them, but Glenn had slowly come to realize something: Kay was usually just feigning her calm, and her real character was actually quite impish.

"Come on, Kay—don't bother the doctor too much," Lorna said.

"That's not something I want to hear from you with that look of yours, Lorna," Kay replied.

Lorna had scolded Kay for her attitude, but it seemed that

seeing Lorna wrapped up in restraints was a difficult sight for Kay, after all. Glenn wondered what she could be thinking, seeing her partner's body wrapped up in so many belts and straps.

"That's awfully condescending for someone who's been injured," Lorna said.

"You troubled the doctor for his help, too, didn't you?"

Before Glenn could stop them, a quiet argument began to develop between them.

Glenn changed out the compress on Kay's leg and tightly wrapped a bandage around it. He did this so that slight movements of her body wouldn't disturb the area affected by the sprain. When he considered Kay's personality, he thought it was possible she might slip away and try to practice with her sword, so in order to make sure she would be fine even if that did happen, he bandaged her leg excessively.

He found the quarreling of the two servants somehow charming. If they had the physical strength to bicker with each other, it was proof that they were in good health.

"Aren't all of those belts too tight?" Kay said. "Is that what you're into, then?"

"Kay, this is something the doctor has done for me. If anybody's 'into it,' it would be him."

"Huh?" Glenn said.

"Oh, is that so?" Kay turned to Glenn. "If that were so, Doctor, you should have told us."

"Right?" Lorna said.

"Um, not, that's..." The conversation had moved in an

uncomfortable direction.

The moment he thought this, he was embraced from behind by Lorna. Suddenly he found himself close to being pushed down into Kay's chest, which was directly in front of him. Lying sprawled out in the straw, Kay could easily take Glenn in despite being injured. Given how much a centaur weighed, it was simple for them to support a single human's body weight.

Kay's breasts were slightly smaller than Tisalia's, but from a human's perspective, they were plenty voluptuous enough.

"We still haven't thanked you—right, Doctor? For treating us..."

"I've already received payment from Tisalia, actually..."

"That's not nearly enough...right? As a thank you, you can do whatever you want to Lorna."

Glenn was sandwiched between the two similar-looking centaurs, front and back.

This is bad, Glenn thought.

The situation was bound to cause misunderstandings if anyone saw it, and the one who hated these types of things most of all was Saphentite. Glenn was sure she was passing medicine to another patient in a separate room of the clinic, but...they were still in the same building, so he knew that she would quickly take notice of what was going on.

Caught in between the two arena fighters, there was no way he could escape.

"With Lorna as she is now, she won't put up any resistance," Kay said.

"That's right, with all these restraints on me—you know?"

The two of them spoke nothing but lies. Lorna's arms and legs were completely free, and she had been caring for Tisalia even with her blindfold on. Restraints or no, Lorna would have no problem punishing any sort of insolent wretch that came her way or put up a fight. And yet they were still saying these things to Glenn.

"Hnh, wouldn't Tisalia...be mad?" he said desperately.

"Tee hee."

"Heh...heh heh heh."

Glenn had hoped that bringing their mistress's name into the conversation would have good results, but the two only laughed at him.

"Our mistress would be mad?"

"That's right," Glenn said. "If she found out, it would be a little awkward, wouldn't it? She does everything fair and square, after all."

"Fair and square?" Kay asked.

"Yes, in battle," Lorna replied.

"And in love," Kay added.

Glenn agreed. If anything, that aspect of her was part of her charm. She confronted everything she faced head-on.

"That's our mistress's virtue, but..." Kay trailed off.

"It's really not suited for matters of the heart, is it?" Lorna asked.

Glenn swallowed. "Wh-what's that supposed to mean?"

"If our mistress...if she marries you, Doctor..."

"We'll also become *your* servants, too, won't we?"

Not that I have any intention of doing that, Glenn thought to himself.

Tisalia often asked Glenn to conduct a marriage interview with her. He always turned her down, saying he was too busy with medical work, but there was a persistence about her that made it seem like she would eventually get her way.

Following up on her words, Kay took Glenn's hand. With a swift motion, she slipped his hand underneath her clothes. He felt silky smooth skin and soft hair brush his fingertips. He thought it must be her stomach.

Indeed, Kay was sliding Glenn's hand across her hourglass stomach. He felt the interchanging human skin and chestnut hair, a texture almost impossible to feel on a human's body. To Glenn, it seemed as if he were being drawn in by the sensation.

"Hn... Phuh." The breath came from one of the two centaurs—or maybe even both of them—and brushed his ear.

"In our culture, servants are the property of their masters."

"If you became husband and wife, you would jointly own each other's property."

The laws of Lindworm gave proper rights to servants—but it seemed that this was not the case in centaur culture. There were some contexts in which monsters prioritized the rules of their own species over the laws of the city—a favoring that sometimes resulted in altercations and caused trouble.

For example, Glenn thought, *like right now.*

"Servants become joint property of the husband and wife..."

"And the servants of the wife also serve the husband."

"In other words, sooner or later we will be your property, Doctor."

"I wouldn't mind if you got a taste while you can."

"Rather, if we *did* let you get a taste..."

"Wouldn't our mistress take it very seriously—a mere doctor laying a hand on one of her servants?"

"Oh, I could see that, see our late-blooming mistress acting that way."

"That's right, if we create a fait accompli situation, then if anything, Dr. Glenn would have no *choice* but to marry our mistress."

The words of the two servants flowed out of their lips one after another, hypnotically.

Their bodies against his felt a little warm, which was no surprise. A centaur's average body temperature was ninety-nine and a half degrees. Thus, for a human like Glenn, it felt a little warm. Squished between the two, he felt like he was breaking into a fever.

"So you see, Doctor..."

"This is all actually for our mistress's sake."

Glenn was seriously in trouble. With this in mind, he reflexively shook them off and escaped from Lorna, standing behind him. He'd thought she would pin him down, but instead she simply let him go.

Seeing both of them giggle, Glenn knew at once that they had been teasing him.

"It was just a joke, Doctor."

"That's right—please don't take it seriously."

"...That was a little bit of a mean prank to pull," he said.

"We're sorry."

"We won't do it again."

"I hope so," he said, wondering how much he could put his trust in them.

Tisalia only did things fair and square, but he couldn't say the same of her two attendants. They both appeared ladylike, but Kay was surprisingly active, and though Lorna was a worrier, she was quick to think on her feet. Glenn now knew they weren't as quiet and well-behaved as they appeared.

"But please don't forget," Kay said.

"We'll do anything and everything for the sake of our mistress, you know?" Lorna said, finishing the sentence.

Glenn wanted to bury his head in his hands.

He was already nervous about avoiding Tisalia's forward, pushy marriage interview invitations. If her two servants joined in with her, he would run out of ways to escape completely.

He wondered if it had *ever* been possible for him to escape the three veteran arena fighters in the first place. That said, if he did agree to a marriage interview, he had no clue just how angry Sapphee might get. And if word got to Cthulhy as well, the continued existence of the clinic could very well be in danger.

Glen could imagine Kay and Lorna, in front of him now, saying that if he couldn't be a doctor anymore, then he could finally be adopted into the Scythia family.

"Someday, the time will come when you become our master."

"Are you excited for that to happen, Doctor?"

Glenn could only give a twitching, forced smile at the grinning faces of the two women in front of him.

It seemed that the master wasn't the only one interested in Glenn—her servants appeared to be interested now, too. The fact itself made him happy, but...

Glenn thought that, at the very least, he should try to ask Tisalia—ask her to keep a firm grip on her servants' reins...and try not to let go.

Although they seemed obedient and quiet, Glenn was sure the awfully unruly pair of horsewomen wouldn't easily be kept under control.

MONSTER GIRL DOCTOR

CASE 02:
The Harpy Who Couldn't Fly

"**I**T SEEMS THAT Illy has agreed to meet with you," the village elder said.

It had been around half a month since Glenn had come to the harpy village.

Kay's sprain had gotten much better, and she had already been discharged from Glenn's clinic. It didn't change the fact that she needed to stay in bed, but now she was helping out with some simple chores in the house that Tisalia was borrowing.

Lorna was still the only one who accompanied Tisalia when she went out, but at this rate, it was quite likely that Kay would soon be able to accompany her as well. Glenn thought it was perfect timing for her completed recovery to coincide with their descent from the mountain.

However, there was a problem with his plan.

The biggest reason for his visit to the village—examining the harpy girl, Illy—had yet to be dealt with. Glenn couldn't leave the village until he had gotten a chance to give her an examination.

Accordingly, he had continued to run his clinic in the village until she was ready for his examination, but—

"Not long ago, she told me she wouldn't mind seeing you."

"Is that true?"

The elder gave a deep nod.

Glenn had been summoned to the old harpy's home. It was a wooden structure like the rest but had a splendid style that was appropriate for a village elder's dwelling. When he heard the summons was regarding Illy, Glenn had told Sapphee, and they had rushed over to see the elder. However—

"But only under certain conditions."

"...Conditions?"

The village elder's keen eyes glanced to Glenn's side.

It seemed that Glenn wasn't the only one who he had called on. Next to him, looking as though a question mark were rising above her head, was Tisalia.

"That's right," the elder said. "Per her stipulations, she wants to have the Scythia's daughter accompany you."

"What, me...?" The color of confusion became steadily more pronounced on Tisalia's face.

She had been in continuous negotiations with the harpy village elder in order to establish an air delivery branch of Scythia Transportation. From what Glenn had heard from Lorna, the business negotiations were going smoothly and documents had been exchanged between Tisalia and the village elder. As the daughter of the company, her business was, for the most part, over.

All that was left was to wait until Kay's injury healed, after which they would descend the mountain with Glenn and the others.

Glenn was sure the centaur's horsepower would be necessary, even though they were going down the mountain this time. Tisalia and her servants were also waiting until Glenn's clinical work in the village was over, but when it came to her own duties, it seemed like there wasn't anything more for her to do in the village, and Glenn had caught her sunbathing or enjoying the hot springs a few times as of late.

"Are you acquainted at all with Miss Illy, Miss Tisalia?" Glenn asked.

"Back when I thought you were in danger and rushed to save you, but...I didn't really see the captured harpies..."

"Yeah, that's right..." he said. Tisalia and her attendants, alongside the other fighters from the arena, had assisted in saving the harpies that had been captured by slave traders. However, she and the others had only driven off slavers that had suddenly attacked Glenn and had not gone directly into the bandits' hideout. Glenn hadn't thought that Illy had even had a chance to learn who Tisalia was. However—

"She most likely heard about her ladyship from the gossip of the other harpy children," the elder said. "My lady is quite conspicuous, after all."

"Does it have something to do with her current disorder?" Glenn asked.

"I don't believe it does..."

So, Illy said she wanted to meet with Tisalia. Glenn agreed with the elder that her request had nothing to do with the ailment that was causing her wing feathers to fall out. Thus, he wondered if it were just because she wanted to meet a centaur, a rare sight to see in the village.

However, even if her condition were just to satisfy her curiosity, it meant Glenn could finally examine Illy, who had—until now—refused his treatment.

"You probably know this, but Illy is still a child," the village elder said gloomily.

It was true. Of all the captured harpies, Illy had been the youngest.

"On top of that, she is worried about her feathers falling out and being unable to fly. Unlike an old bird like me, a young harpy would feel a great deal of anxiety about being unable to fly. If Glenn saw her, maybe she would be more at ease—that's how we saw it, at least."

"Naturally. I will make sure to examine her properly," he answered without a second thought. It was one of the main reasons for Glenn's visit, after all. "But, Miss Tisalia..."

"I will go as well, of course! No matter what shape it may take, if I can be of some use to the doctor, then I'd be more than happy to help."

Tisalia was as dependable as ever.

"Anyway," Glenn said, "I can't examine her without meeting her first. It's fine doing things this way—right, Sapphee?"

"Yes, Doctor. Depending on her condition, she might need medicine, so I will prepare some. However..." Sapphee cast a sidelong glance at Tisalia. Glenn wondered if she were going to say something that would start another quarrel, but with a tranquil look on her face, Sapphee said: "Ignoring whatever reason she had for calling Miss Tisalia, I must say...her coming along might end up actually causing trouble."

"Hold on a second, Miss Sapphee. What does that mean?" Tisalia asked.

"I'm not being sarcastic or trying to suggest anything. The village elder just informed us that Miss Illy is a child, but she *is* fourteen years old... She's going through puberty. What I meant to say is that the heart of a tender-aged young girl isn't something that can be so easily understood."

A silence fell over everyone at Sapphee's words of caution.

Glenn realized Illy was around the same age as Lulala, Lindworm's songstress, whose examination hadn't exactly gone smoothly. Glenn took Sapphee's remarks to heart, telling himself once again that he needed to pull himself together and deal with Illy like a gentlemen.

"In any event, please allow us to meet with her at once," he said. The village elder gave a deep nod at Glenn's request.

✕ ✖ ✖ ✖ ✕

Guided by the young harpies, Glenn arrived where Illy was staying. It was a house even further removed from the others. He had heard that it was a separate cottage used for medical treatment and recovery, so it was quite far from the village.

Illy was already unable to fly and couldn't even go to her house built in the rock wall, but Glenn thought that being so separated from the village was probably especially discouraging for her.

"I suppose a harpy being unable to fly is like a centaur losing their ability to run," Sapphee said.

"Or like a lamia losing the ability to slither," Tisalia replied.

Sapphee and Tisalia both seemed to be hitting the mark, but Glenn thought they were still a little off with their lines of thinking.

Being able to fly was a gift granted only to bugs and birds— and to a number of monsters.

A bird could walk on earth and see things from a human's perspective, but humans could never fly in the air themselves. Thinking about it like that, Glenn was sure that the anguish of a flightless harpy was beyond his comprehension.

That being said, the village elder seemed just fine being unable to fly, so it was possible he was over-thinking things, and yet...

"Excuse me." Pushing open the plain wooden door, Glenn entered the cottage.

The inside of the room was dark. The cottage didn't seem to be in an area that got a lot of sun, and there wasn't any sort of illumination inside the room itself.

Glenn strained his eyes to search for Illy, however it wasn't a silhouette that he glimpsed in the darkness.

It was white feathers.

"This is..."

White feathers were scattered all over the floor of the cottage. There were gray and black ones mixed in as well, though they didn't stand out in the dark. Glenn picked up one of the feathers on reflex. It had fallen out, but not so long ago, as the tips were still standing straight up.

"A flight feather!" Long and sturdy. Looking at the magnificent feather, Glenn immediately came to a conclusion.

When a harpy opened up both its arms, these feathers were the ones that extended out the most from its body. Birds had the same types of feather, and they worked effectively to grant flight. If these feathers fell out, the harpy's balance would be ruined, making it hard to fly. Birds bred in captivity had these flight feathers intentionally clipped to ensure they couldn't escape—that was just how important these feathers were for flying.

Glenn thought that it would be troublesome to clean everything up, so he left the feathers where they were. He peered into the murk and caught sight of a shadow in the back of the room with a blanket over its head.

The shadow was peeking at Glenn through a gap in the blanket.

"Nice to see you again," Glenn greeted the shadow. Behind him, Sapphee bowed, while Tisalia gave a wave, smiling brightly.

"Do you remember me? I'm Glenn Litbeit, the doctor who treated you before. Have you been doing well since then?"

"...Does it look like I'm doing well?"

"You raise a good point—your condition appears to be quite serious, doesn't it?" Glenn sighed. When he considered how she'd been cooped up in this unclean, messy shack, he got the feeling that her environment was doing more to bring her down mentally than her illness was.

Illy poked her head out from underneath the blanket. Before, while treating her impacted oviduct, Glenn hadn't had a chance to get a good look at her face, but looking at her now, he could see she had strong-willed features. He assumed the red irritation at the corner of her eyes had come from crying.

Sapphee had found a broom and seemed intent on cleaning up the shack. Tisalia, ever herself, opened up the windows and started ventilating the space. Something had been covering the panes, Glenn realized.

"Is that Miss Tisalia?" Illy asked.

"That's right," Glenn replied. "She's come along just as you asked. You had something you needed from her?"

"Well, yeah..." Illy's attitude was curt and blunt.

Glenn didn't think they'd be welcome after she had refused to see him up until yesterday, but her gaze was fixed on Tisalia, who had begun to help Sapphee with her cleaning.

"Will you let me examine you?" Glenn asked.

"Sure... Hey, Doctor, what's wrong with me?"

"That's what I'm going to try and find out now. Is that okay with you?"

"Okay..."

Glenn was starting to think that this might be a more challenging case than he had expected.

Illy didn't look Glenn in the eye even once. He felt unsure about how best to handle a young girl going through puberty. Even her replies to his questions were curt and brusque.

"For now, I'm going to take off the blanket."

"Whatever."

Glenn stripped away the blanket Illy was wrapped in.

She was a young girl with impressive red hair. It had been disheveled when she was a captive of the slave traders, but now it was properly combed. The hair on the top of her head stood up, but Glenn knew that was just from the feathers that made up her crest. There were also fluffy down feathers extending from the front all the way around to the back of her neck.

What really stood out, however, were her arms and legs.

From both of her upper limbs, which were equitable to human arms, she had the signature wings of a harpy. The underlying color of her feathers was red like her hair, but the outer stretches of her wings, her flight feathers, were a gradation of white to black. Among the diversely colored wings of the harpy, the color tone of her wings was somewhat on the subdued side of the spectrum.

However, Illy's wings seemed relatively big in comparison to her body. Glenn felt that she must have had quite the ability to fly.

Her legs had sharp talons like a falcon. Glenn thought absently to himself that it would hurt to be kicked by her. It seemed highly likely that the young harpy girl would attack with these talons if she tried to resist the examination, so he made a mental note to be careful of her kicks.

"Please stand and spread out your wings for me, please."

"Okay."

Illy thrust out her wings. Just as Glenn had thought, they were quite big compared to her body.

The shapes and sizes of certain monster species—including harpies—could vary depending on the region where they lived. The differences between these subspecies could be quite intense. For example, while the centaur subspecies might only differ in size and coat color, the differences between subspecies of mermaids and harpies could be quite dramatic.

Harpies had particularly varied characteristics, due to the many colors and shapes their feathers could take, as well as the varying sizes of their wings and the many shapes of their crests. Individual feather colors were mainly passed down through their parents but in practice, a diverse combination of colors and shapes could be seen, enough so that it was said no two harpies shared the same plumage.

Some raptor-like harpies looked like owls and hawks, while other harpies resembled ground-walking birds like ostriches and chickens, and others still lived seabird lifestyles on the shores and islands of the world. Even so, it was nevertheless possible to broadly categorize all the different subspecies of harpy. However, since all the different subspecies were able to marry and have children with one another, this also meant there was a possibility that their individual characteristics would be mixed together in the children they produced.

Glenn wondered what sort of characteristics her parents had

passed down to her, to give her this appearance.

"Hmph... Make it quick," Illy said.

Glenn first began touching the base of her wings—what would have been her upper arms had she been human. It was near this area that harpies' arms transformed into bird wings. Glenn closely observed the area where skin transformed into feather. However, there wasn't anything especially out of the ordinary. The base of the wing was sensitive, though; it was a place where dormant pathogens could easily lurk.

"I'm going touch them now, okay?"

"Hm... Ah, uuunh."

Illy stirred slightly but didn't give any other indication that she wanted Glenn to stop touching her. He began stroking her wings, but there wasn't anything unusual there either.

"I'm going to go a bit further in now."

"Ah! Hnh!"

Glenn started to force his finger into Illy's wing.

With a majority of her flight feathers having fallen out, the density of feathers on her wings was weak, and Glenn quickly reached the surface of Illy's skin beneath the feathers. The areas where her feathers had fallen out felt like rough bird skin, but that in and of itself was normal. Indeed, Glenn founding nothing that was particularly unusual.

He wondered if there weren't some other area of her wings exhibiting signs of strangeness and again began slipping his fingers into her feathers.

"Make sure to let me know if it hurts."

"That much doesn't hurt... Hn, hng."

There wasn't any swelling or bleeding.

When Glenn had heard her feathers were falling out, his first thought had been some kind of skin disease. Yet Illy's skin was firm and appeared to be healthy. He couldn't see a rash or anything of that nature. He even tried touching the skin on the tips of her wings and still found no irregularities.

"Miss Illy, do your wings feel itchy or painful at all?" he asked.

"Not really..."

There were no external injuries, either.

Even humans would experience swelling and hair loss if they were bruised on their head. Glenn had thought Illy might be dealing with something similar, but as she had no injuries, he felt it was safe to exclude that possibility.

He again felt through her wing with his finger and this time began examining around the glossy, red down that had yet to fall out. It was protected with a moderate coating of oils and fat. In fact, her down feathers were in excellent condition. Harpy feather quills and bedding were actually considered very high-quality merchandise. In addition to being superb at keeping in warmth, harpy down's softness was something other materials had a hard time imitating.

"I'm going to pull on them a little, okay?"

"Hurry up." Illy was thoroughly cold and short in her reply. Glenn had been troubled by Lulala's extreme degree of embarrassment when he had examined her, but this cold reception and level of indifference made it just as difficult for Glenn in its own way.

"Nh—ah!"

"Does it hurt?"

"It's fine..."

Even when he pulled on the red down feathers, they showed no sign of falling out. This wasn't surprising, though, as it was only a specific portion of her feathers that were falling out—the strong and sturdy flight feathers on the outer part of her wings.

Through these examinations, Glenn determined that it was extremely unlikely her ailment was caused by some kind of skin disease.

It was possible that stress was causing her to lose her feathers, but they had a lustrous sheen to them and were in good health. Considering things from a mental health perspective as well, Glenn was sure that her time with the slave traders had been far more stressful than her current situation.

"...Hm."

"What?"

"Do you have an appetite? Are you eating properly?"

"Hmph." Illy took something out from the pouch on her waist, a handful of lightly roasted nuts. Skillfully taking them with her wings, Illy began to chow down on them. "I only eat these. That a problem?"

"No, that's fine. You don't need to force yourself to eat right here and now."

Glenn interpreted it to mean that she had an appetite but couldn't eat anything substantial. Harpies preferred to eat nuts and beans, anyway. It didn't mean there was anything wrong with her diet or eating habits.

She could have just told me that, Glenn thought to himself.

He wondered if there was some meaning behind her physically showing Glenn that she could eat, or if it were simply because she was a bad talker.

"Can you show me your head?"

"Huh, why?"

"I want to look at your crest."

In response to the abrupt proposition, Illy glared at Glenn.

Glenn tried his best not to frighten her and returned her glare with a bright smile, but Illy quickly stooped forward and presented her head to Glenn. She glared at him with her upturned eyes; it appeared she was staying on her guard.

Glenn wondered why she was acting so hostile towards him in the first place. He couldn't recall doing anything to cause her to be so displeased with him.

"I'm going to touch it now."

"Mhm..." Illy brought her wings up to her face and made a strange expression.

The crest that bobbed on top of her head was a greyish red. At first glance, it looked like just a piece of her hair sticking up, but the crest didn't grow out of her skin like hair and instead was connected to her bones. As such—

"Hn."

To some extent, Illy could move it up and down of her own free will.

A harpy's crest had a number of different roles, from signaling one's presence to one's friends, to making one attractive to the opposite sex—but as Illy was able to move it a bit, it appeared there weren't any problems with hers.

"Does it hurt?"

"It... i-it tickles..."

Glenn had a hard time getting a hold of the crest as it bobbed to and fro.

He had a sudden, unconscious urge to chase after and play with her bouncing crest, but that would clearly have been going beyond what his position required, and he managed to control himself. He also felt bad when he saw how itchy Illy seemed to be and took his hand off of her head.

"Now then, last up is this."

Glenn slid his hands down her body.

"H-hyaaaah?!"

At Illy's sharp cry, both Tisalia and Sapphee looked up from their cleaning towards Glenn.

"Oh, sorry! Stay still for me, okay?"

"Y-yo—ah! All of a sudden...! Huah?!"

"Allow me to take your temperature."

"S-say that first... Aaaagh!"

Glenn's fingertips were in Illy's armpit. The clinic had mercury thermometers, but they were quick to break, and the readings they gave were unreliable. As a higher-performance thermometer had not yet been developed, his most reliable method for taking temperatures was using his intuition and experience.

Out of the corner of his eye, Glenn could see Sapphee sink down as she let out a sigh. She clearly thought he had made a mess of things again, somehow or other, but there wasn't any way he could put a stop to it now.

Illy's shoulders and armpits were bare, a trait common among all harpies. Considering the structure of their wings, sleeves would have only gotten in the way.

"Hyahn!"

"Please don't move."

"Th-they're—they're cold!"

"Yes, I'm sure my hands must feel cold to you. Harpies have a naturally high internal body temperature."

"Urrrrggghhhh!"

Illy struggled, her face turning red, but Glenn had given her a strict order not to move. If she shifted the wrong way, the accuracy of Glenn's temperature reading would go down.

As if she had finally resigned herself to what was going on, Illy tiredly dropped her wings and stopped resisting Glenn.

"One-hundred-point-four degrees. No problems with your body temperature... Thank you, that concludes the examination."

"Doctor!" Sapphee said. "Didn't I tell you to be considerate!"

"Gwah!" Glenn, caught by an outstretched snake tail, involuntarily let out a strange noise.

Glenn thought that this time he was absolutely in the wrong and resigned himself to Sapphee's chastising. She let go and dropped Glenn to the floor as if saying she had given up and thus conveyed her anger to him.

"Oh my, Doctor—are you okay?" Tisalia asked. "That snake woman is quite violent, isn't she?"

"I don't want to hear that from a horsewoman who can only solve things with her spear!" Sapphee retorted.

"Both of you, take it easy. We're still in front of the patient."

Even when tangled up in Sapphee's tail, Glenn remained calm and collected.

Illy had a somewhat pouting look in her eyes, but she kept staring straight at Glenn. Her eyes looked serious and earnest. Glenn knew this look very well. They were the eyes of a patient waiting for the results of an examination. Eyes that fearfully asked what sickness was hiding itself in their body.

"Doctor...what kind of disease is this?"

"It's not a disease." Glenn spoke in as gentle a voice as possible.

"You're not sick. Your feathers are falling because you're molting. This happens with the change of the season... The feathers that have fallen out will regrow soon. Don't worry."

Just as many animals shed their summer fur for a warmer winter coat, harpies molted to adequately greet the change of seasons. There wasn't any problem with her physical health, and there wasn't any wear and tear on her feathers from stress. In addition to that, since there weren't any external injuries or skin damage, it meant that this problem of hers wasn't from any sickness or disease. It was just a normal physiological phenomenon.

"You should make sure to eat properly and rest well to try and get your ability to fly back as soon as possible."

"...You're lying." Illy bit her lips. She was looking down so Glenn couldn't see her expression, but she seemed frustrated, somehow. "That's not true."

"I'm not lying. You're not sick."

"I'm not sick?! What?! That can't be! I've never had any-thing like this happen before! Sure, my feathers always fall out and come back at the end of the season but...I was still able to fly when that happened! Up until now I could *always* fly! There's no way molting would make me unable to fly!"

She could no longer fly because this time, even her flight feathers were molting. Harpy wings were very delicate and just losing two or three feathers could have an immediate effect on their ability to fly.

"More feathers are falling out than normal, that's all. It hap-pens sometimes. Losing the ability to fly from molting is some-thing that often happens to harpies—"

"You're wrong! I've never stopped being able to fly from something like this! It's not normal!"

"But you're not sick..."

"Whatever!" Illy stamped her feet in frustration and annoyance.

Glenn couldn't hazard a guess as to why she had gotten so hysterical. Had she been hoping she was sick? He had a feeling that wasn't exactly the case.

"I'm not listening to you anymore, you quack! I didn't even want to see you! I hate all of you!"

"Hold on a sec, Illy. Now, calm down a sec and listen— "

"...!"

What happened next Glenn felt was probably something she did on reflex.

He approached her, thinking that he should try and calm her down. However, possibly due to his thoughtless method for measuring her temperature a few minutes prior, a frightened look came to Illy's face, and she brandished her legs at Glenn.

Her raptor legs, which ended in sharp talons could easily rend through human flesh. Glenn stood captivated by the claws as they lunged towards him from below, like a scythe.

"Pardon me," Tisalia said, stopping their approach with a broomstick extended in front of Illy's legs. If things had kept going in the direction they'd been headed, Glenn's face would have been deeply cut. Tisalia remained perfectly calm and wedged herself between the two, protecting Glenn from Illy's talons as if she were dealing with a child.

"This bird's got quite a bad kicking habit, doesn't she?" she said.

"Hmph! Grrrrrrrrr!" Illy's face was bright red. She looked as if she didn't know whether to be angry or to cry, and stood there trembling for a moment, until she finally dashed past Tisalia.

"Hey—wait, Illy!" Glenn called after her.

There was no chance to stop her.

Illy was surprisingly fast as she ran off on foot. It was enough to make Glenn think that with legs that fast, there wasn't any need for her to fly through the sky in the first place.

"Now what to do..."

"You're far too tactless, Doctor." Sapphee didn't hesitate to heap another blow on the already dejected Glenn. However, she too looked troubled as she rubbed the scales at the sides of her eyes. "Even so...I do feel that there was something off. No matter how inconsiderate you may be, was it really necessary for her to get that mad?"

Glenn was of a similar mind. He had a feeling that the reason she was annoyed and angry had nothing to do with what he had done—but if that were the case, then what *was* her reason? Glenn was sure he hadn't been incorrect in his diagnosis but wondered if perhaps he hadn't been able to properly explain it to her.

"Anyway, let's head after her. We don't know where she might end up in her current state," he said.

"That's right—we have to hurry."

Harpies were known to do things their own way even under normal circumstances, and other races of monsters often called them oblivious and forgetful, but the cause of that lay in their excitable personality. There was a good chance Illy might do something unexpected out of desperation. Her species had a tendency to become sidetracked and fixated, ignoring everything else around them when they were seized by one thing in particular.

Glenn couldn't help but wonder what might happen given how upset she'd been.

"Doctor, may I say something?" Tisalia asked, handing the broom she used to defend Glenn from Illy's claws over to Sapphee. "Wouldn't chasing after her right now just make things worse?"

"Y-you might be right..."

"Forgive me if this is presumptuous, but..." Tisalia's stare was fixed in the direction that Illy had run toward. "Can you leave this up to me? As luck would have it, I'm rather confident in the strength of my legs." Stooping down and rubbing her front legs, she smiled graciously.

× × ✖ ✖ ×

It was easy for Tisalia Scythia to chase after Illy.

Illy was, in fact, quite fast. Nevertheless, there wasn't any monster that had legs capable of outrunning a centaur on open ground.

Running out of the quarantined cottage, the tracks of a harpy's talons were punctured in the earth like foot prints. This was the evidence Illy had left behind when she forcibly stomped away, unable to take off and fly.

The tracks Tisalia followed ended at the banks of the river that flowed through the town. Along these banks, the harpies piled up felled timber from around the village for safekeeping. Using this lumber, the harpies built their splendid homes, whether on the ground or into the sides of the precipitous cliffs above.

Illy was lingering around this lumber storage area.

She gave Tisalia a sharp glare. "...Just you? What about the doctor?"

"I thought that even if he did come, you wouldn't listen to what he said anyway."

"So, you *do* get it."

"You had some business with me, correct?"

Tisalia Scythia had frequently felt a pair of eyes staring at her while spending time in the village. Illy had most likely been out and about in the village and had just made sure to keep to areas where Glenn wouldn't see her. Tisalia wasn't sure what had caused Illy to be so interested in her. Whatever the reason, she had been examined by Glenn in order to meet with Tisalia.

"Quite a roundabout way of going about it," the centaur said. "If you wanted to meet with me, you could have just asked directly."

"The elder told me...that if I wanted to talk with the Scythian heiress, I needed to be properly looked at beforehand... Not that it mattered, anyway."

"I see."

In other words, Tisalia thought, this had been the elder's strategy all along. That eagle-like elder looked to be taking it easy, but it seemed that he was actually quite shrewd.

"Y-you're an arena fighter, right?" Illy asked.

"Yes... And?"

Tisalia found it insolent of Illy to address a monster she had only just met with "you," but she tried as hard as possible to answer calmly. She admonished herself in her head, thinking it would be unreasonably immature to be angered by the words of a child.

"I've gone to see a lot of matches," Illy said. "I'd ditch my work here in the village and fly down and stand on the pillars in the arena. You can see the fights for free there—did you know that?"

"Naturally, if even paying customers can't sit up there, I don't care if you paid or not."

It was certainly a special privilege of those who could fly. The pillars that surrounded the arena were about the same height as a church's steeple. The only people who could easily get up to those seats were harpies and other monsters capable of flight.

As an arena fighter, however, Tisalia wasn't impressed to hear Illy boldly brag that she watched the arena fights for free.

"I can't fly anymore... Now that I'm like this."

"I still don't see where you're coming from. What exactly are you trying to say?"

"I want to be like you." Illy looked Tisalia straight in the eyes, her own eyes sparkling.

Tisalia was pretty sure this was the first time she'd seen Illy raise her head up, the harpy girl who had stared morosely at the ground during Glenn's entire examination.

"You're so amazing and brilliant. I didn't know your name or anything, but I thought you were so cool when you were fighting in the arena."

"If you're a fan, then I'd like to thank you. But that isn't the case, is it?"

"I want to do what you do."

Tisalia heaved a sigh. The stars of the arena were its female fighters. It was something Lindworm was known for. There were many, both human and monster, who aspired to such a profession. It was true that the appearance of beauty and battle mixed together was a charming one, and if one became a top-tier fighter, the prestige and rewards for doing so were extraordinary. But of course, an arena fighter wasn't something easy to become.

Although they were all imitations, weapons *were* permitted. And until the referee handed down his judgment of the match, fighters clashed with one another with all of their strength inside the small coliseum. The fights always came with injuries, and the prize money the lower ranked fighters battled for was smaller than the tears of a sparrow. Yet despite that, one's scheduled matches could completely fill up the day.

There was training, as well as a number of tests, that one had to undergo to even become qualified to be a fighter in the first place. Tisalia wondered if Illy was prepared to overcome all of that.

The Scythia clan had made their name known throughout the continent as mercenaries, and yet even the heiress of such a warrior clan was only a rank three fighter. The top rank of the arena was filled with an incredible group of fighters. The sheer, exceptional skill required to reach that pinnacle was evident in the former number one fighter: Kunai Zenow, an undead martial artist who couldn't die even when killed.

"Just wanting to be a fighter doesn't mean you'll be able to become one," Tisalia said.

"I will! This village is too small for me! I used to live in the city slums... I'm much more suited for Lindworm than this little village!"

"You hate the village? Everyone here is nice, right?"

"That's not it. The village elder and everyone else aren't bad people, but...I just... When I skip out on work—and even now when I'm sick and can't fly anymore—they're all still nice to me..."

That's why I can't take it! It's uncomfortable being in a village like this that doesn't even throw out a useless person like me!"

Tisalia thought the village's attitude was a result of the harsh, unforgiving environment that surrounded it, halfway to the summit of the Vivre Mountains. The colony was on the banks of the river, surrounded by precipitous cliffs and was most likely cut off from the world by snow in winter. A mountainside village like this one was supported by its residents all helping each other out. Those who could move would fly to obtain necessary items for the village and bring them back. That was the wisdom of these harpies, who had lived here since before Lindworm had been built.

"I want to go somewhere away from here... I can fly, so I can go anywhere I want."

"Becoming a fighter is no ordinary task. Do you know any martial arts?"

"I can hold my own in a fight! Want me to show you?"

Raising her legs up, Illy gave a ferocious smile. Tisalia imagined it was something she had learned naturally from living in the slums, given the dangerous weapons Illy had been equipped with since birth.

However, Illy's dream was entirely out of the question. Illy was mistaken about both the arena and its fighters. She seemed to think it would be enough to simply win battles and beat her opponent.

"Well, the arena—they'll accept anyone who comes to them, so long as you tell them you want to be a fighter," Tisalia said.

"But if you only go into it half-heartedly, you'll have a terrible time of it. It's a hard thing to hear, but you should give up on it."

"What?! You're just like everyone else! You're saying it's impossible for me, is that it?!"

Tisalia figured that the village elder must have reprimanded her with the same words. Illy was clearly frustrated. She wondered if the harpy's frustrations had anything to do with her feathers falling out. Tisalia had no idea— in fact, that sort of thing was Glenn's territory. It wasn't something for her to think about.

"What goes on in the arena isn't just a fight or a brawl," Tisalia said. "It's a place to compete with beauty and technical skill."

"That's basically just a fight, isn't it?"

"No. I'm saying that first of all, one's character and behavior are important above all else."

Illy tilted her head back and forth as though Tisalia's words weren't really getting through to her.

Tisalia heaved another deep sigh. It seemed to her that no matter what she said to the harpy, she wouldn't get it. Tisalia wasn't particularly good at expressing herself either—or rather, her personality made her think it was faster to use her body to explain things than her words.

"All right, then. I guess I'll accept your challenge. Show me what you've got."

"We're fighting? You're on! Sounds good to me. I'm not gonna be responsible if you get hurt!"

Illy raised her legs and bared her claws.

Tisalia picked up a suitable piece of lumber that was lying

around and readied it like a spear. Illy had trained herself in street brawls against hoodlums in the slums, and Tisalia wondered just how well she would stand her ground against her spear technique.

"First of all, a fighter needs to show courtesy to the audience and their opponent."

Readying her spear of timber, Tisalia realized something: She was angrier at Illy than she had thought.

"To clarify—your manners have been unacceptable from the very start, calling the young man who saved you from slave traders a quack doctor! I'll be sure to punish your insolence. Now, come at me if you dare!"

Illy kicked strongly off the ground and sprung toward Tisalia.

With all the free time she'd had recently, this spur-of-the-moment fighting test was the first good exercise she'd had in a while.

✕ ✕ ✖ ✕ ✕

"...That was quite reckless of you."

Glenn gently dabbed the disinfectant-soaked cotton cloth on Tisalia's cheek.

"O-ow! It huuurts!"

"Just try to bear with it for a moment."

Glenn was treating the line of sharp scratches that ran across Tisalia's face. Knowing that Tisalia devoted herself day in and day out to martial arts in the arena, Glenn couldn't hide his surprise that her face had been injured.

Tisalia had flown into the clinic long after the examinations for the day had been finished. Glenn wondered what kind of battle had played out between her and Illy. Preparing dinner further back in the clinic, Sapphee didn't even attempt to hide the exasperated look of amazement on her face.

"I didn't plan on going easy on her, but...I made a mistake."

"Illy's knowledgeable about fighting? "

"Not at all. The way she fought—it was a vulgar way to brawl. I suppose that's why her claws ended up grazing my cheek..."

In all honesty, Glenn didn't understand anything about fighting.

However, beauty and grace were important assets for female arena fighters. Tisalia took care to maintain a suitable appearance, and even in a street bawl would surely want to avoid any injuries to her face. All that said, it seemed Illy had the fighting capability to graze Tisalia with her attacks.

"Well, even still, I was able to give her a thorough thrashing with that piece of lumber, you know? Oh, ho, ho, ho!"

"You went easy on her, right?"

"Of course. It was nothing more than a little disciplining... I can't deny that I got a bit stubborn about it, though..."

With the gauze stuck to her wounds, Tisalia's treatment was complete. The wound itself wasn't serious, and Glenn was confident it would heal quickly without leaving a scar. The problem was with Illy.

Tisalia said she had gone easy on the young harpy girl, but Illy had still been hit with a piece of lumber, so it wasn't out of the question for her to have a bruise or two. Glenn wanted to examine her as well, if possible, but it was hard for him to believe she would obediently let him take a look at her injuries.

"What'd you think would come of fighting with a young girl like that, anyway?"

"Really!" Sapphee said, cutting into their conversation.

Tisalia sulked as if she were making an excuse for herself. "I lost my cool because she insulted Dr. Glenn."

It was a fair enough defense—being a rather skilled physician, Glenn didn't exactly merit being referred to as a quack.

"In fact, Miss Sapphee," Tisalia went on, "she insulted the doctor, right? Shouldn't *you* be the one to get angry and tell her off?"

"Oh, I'm angry all right," Sapphee said. "Right now, I'm thinking about how to make that young harpy drink some anesthetic."

"You don't hold anything back, do you...?"

"It was just a joke." Sapphee kept a composed look as she made her outrageous statements. Well-versed in pharmaceutical and assassination techniques, she was certainly capable of carrying out her threats if she really wanted to—a frightening thought, indeed.

"Anyway, we can't just leave Illy alone," Glenn said. "We have to do something."

"But Doctor? She isn't sick at all, right?" Tisalia asked.

"That's the problem..."

Glenn put his head in his hands. Illy was molting—just growing new feathers. He was *sure* that was case. The shedding and regrowth of feathers or fur in accordance with the changing of the seasons was a trait shared by many monsters. Illy's symptoms matched a molting diagnosis.

"Is there any chance your diagnosis was incorrect?"

"Even if that were the case, I can't think of any other illness she might have..."

It would be a serious matter if Glenn had overlooked some sign of illness, but he couldn't recall anything that like that in his examination. Had he missed something crucial? As a doctor, it was always a possibility. He was still relatively inexperienced and because of that, he always felt the need to doubt and double-check his conclusions.

"I think Illy's problem is that there's something wrong with the girl herself," Tisalia said.

The centaur was strangely worried about Illy for some reason. Glenn wondered if it was because Illy was an orphan like her two attendants, Kay and Lorna. Tisalia was truly a very compassionate centaur princess.

"She said she originally lived in the slums," Tisalia said. "Her new life is a big change from what she was used to, so maybe that's why she's trying to run away. Or more likely, she is still trying to live as she did back then. Her wings *would* make it easy to move from place to place, looking for somewhere she feels at home... It's probably that wild lifestyle, always alone, with no one to rely on, that attracted the slave traders to her in the first place."

"You think that's why she's saying she wants to become a fighter, too?" Glenn wondered.

"It's just a nice excuse so she can run away from here," Tisalia replied. "Honestly, I'd rather she didn't make light of us fighters like that."

Glenn thought that since she had lived and survived by relying on her fighting skills, it made sense that she wouldn't quite be able to adjust to the relaxed atmosphere in the village.

There were other harpies besides Illy who had been captured by the slave traders. However, these other young girls occupied themselves with their work without skipping out or slacking off. They had just recently come to the clinic to greet Glenn and Sapphee. Considering this, Illy was the only one who was unable to adapt to life in the village.

"If it really is her molt..." Sapphee began.

"So long as her flight feathers return, she'll be able to fly again. If that happens, she might decide to fly away from the village for good this time," Glenn said.

"...You might be right."

"Seeing how she acted, I wouldn't be surprised if she became desperate."

She'd fly away, off to somewhere far away from here?

If she did, there was a chance that she might be captured again by people like the slave traders who'd taken her before. They had handled the harpies with care in their own way, but Glenn was sure that kind of care among traders was far from normal. Threats to her life and chastity were lying in wait everywhere.

Glenn's thoughts were getting bleaker and bleaker.

Even though it was almost certain that she wasn't sick, the

other circumstances surrounding her made Glenn and the others' heads fill with worry.

"If I just knew what subspecies Illy was..." he said.

"Subspecies?" Tisalia asked.

"The subspecies of harpy. Compared with other monsters, harpies have many different subspecies, and each has unique ways of living and illnesses they can contract. With her large wings and strong talons—well, I think it's pretty clear she has some high-soaring raptor subspecies in her veins, but..."

Her dislike of being tied down to one place might not just be a part of Illy herself but instead could be a characteristic of her subspecies. Her quick-to-fight temperament was another trait often seen in raptor subspecies.

"That girl's an orphan, right? She did say something about not knowing her lineage," Tisalia said.

"During your fight?"

"Well, I kind of got her to say as much."

Glenn thought that if he knew what type of wings Illy's parents had, he would understand why she wasn't able to fly. But if she didn't know her own lineage, then he couldn't hold out hope on that front.

"That, and I have this." Tisalia drew a single feather from her breast pocket.

"It's one of Illy's—it fell out in the middle of our battle... I thought it was particularly big. Could it help your diagnosis?"

"I'll have a look." Glenn took the feather and stared at it closely.

It was a deep gray. The color changed to a jet black at the feather's tip. It was quite long, even when compared to other big and sturdy flight feathers. Glenn thought that it must have come from the section of flight feathers known as the primary flight feathers.

The feather had no flaws and a beautiful gray sheen to it. It was plain but with a stained tinge of color. There didn't seem to be anything wrong with the feathers that were falling out, so it really did seem that Illy was in good health. Yet—

"...?"

There was a section on the feather that nearly blended in with all the gray, but Glenn still caught sight of it: a spot at the base of the feather where it was turning red.

Though there had been a number of red feathers at the base of her wing, Glenn had been sure her flight feathers were all essentially black or gray.

A red-winged harpy.

Glenn thought to himself, then said, "...Sapphee?"

"Yes, what is it?"

"Can you help me out a little tomorrow?"

"Of course. Anytime, anywhere."

There was nothing more reassuring than his partner's immediate answer, given without knowing any of the details of Glenn's request. Then he realized that she was using both her hands and the top of her tail to hold plates and carry them. Glenn thought she must be hinting that it was time for dinner.

"What are you going to do?" she asked.

"Yes, well, you see," Glenn said as he twirled the feather in his hand, "we're going to have a treasure hunt through the village."

✖ ✖ ✖ ✖ ✖

Glenn wanted to search for Illy's feathers—as many as they could find.

He and Sapphee set out searching for the feathers together. However, they were in a harpy village—there was a considerable number of feathers to be found on the roads, as harpies lost a number of feathers over the course of a normal day. Among all these feathers, they had to collect only those that belonged to Illy.

The work was rather time-consuming.

Sapphee held up her parasol as she helped Glenn. However, he didn't want to expose the albino lamia to the rays of the sun, so he had her collect feathers indoors as much as he could.

For the most part, Glenn was the one running around outside collecting feathers—along with the help of Tisalia and her capable legs. As expected of the horsewoman, her physical fitness was above average; she rushed to every corner of the village and collected all of the feathers that appeared to belong to Illy.

After spending the whole day on the task, they had collected quite a bundle of feathers. In the village's open square, Glenn used a magnifying glass to examine them in detail.

"How is this, Doctor?" Tisalia asked.

"Thank you, Miss Tisalia."

Since coming to the village, he had done nothing but rely

upon both Sapphee and Tisalia's strengths.

After examining the feather, Glenn could see that his guess was correct. No matter what type of feather he looked at, they were all turning faintly red at the shaft. Not only that, but he could see highly saturated tinges of yellows and blues, as well. He wondered what it meant.

"Do you think you've figured something out?" Tisalia spoke to Glenn as if she were trying to get into his thoughts as he focused all of his attention on the feathers.

"Yes...probably—if my hunch is correct..."

"It's some kind of illness, different from molting?"

"No, it's molting. That is a fact."

"...?" Tisalia tilted her head.

It wasn't a misdiagnosis—Glenn was certain that Illy's symptoms were a result of molting. However, what he was thinking of was something subtly different from molting. He was positive that if he could properly convey that subtle difference to Illy without her misinterpreting him, she would finally understand.

"You're confident, aren't you, Doctor?"

"Does it look that way?" Glenn was often told he looked timid and unsure, and rarely heard someone say the opposite.

"Yes, you do. After all, you're making the same face the fighters in the arena make—a face completely free of indecision. The warriors who face their matches with such a look usually end up winning, you know."

Being compared to the renowned fighters of the arena was a great honor.

Tisalia combed a hand through her hair and gave a somewhat lonely smile. Looking at her up close, Glenn thought that she was certainly worthy of the many fans she had as a fighter, what with her graceful and shapely features. Bending her body down and bringing her face close to Glenn's, she made his heart skip a beat, even with their familiar relationship.

"Illy said it herself," Tisalia said. "'Being here makes me want to go somewhere else.'"

"Hm? Like where...?"

"Who knows? I'm sure there is somewhere that has what this place lacks. That's what she's thinking, that girl."

An escape—that was what Illy sought. Flying and escaping were similar in nature, after all. The sky was freedom, without anything to hold one down—he wondered if there was something that Illy could get only from being up high in the sky, at heights Tisalia and Glenn could not reach.

"The only one who understands her pain from being unable to fly is Illy herself," Tisalia said.

"That's right..."

"It's... it's because I'm not smart. When I was a kid, I neglected my studies to exercise with my spear. That's why I didn't have any argument or debating skills with which to discourage that girl... When it comes to scolding a child, all I can do is make them understand by knocking them down with a weapon. That girl is foolish, but so am I." Tisalia was worrying over the harpy girl as if Illy were her younger sister.

Sapphee made a similar face at times when she was talking

to Glenn. She might now refer to him as "Doctor," but for her, Glenn was still a kind of little brother to her.

"But... Miss Tisalia, you're still worried about Illy," Glenn said.

"It's not enough." Tisalia shook her head. "Worrying about something won't help or save anyone. But with your extensive knowledge, Doctor, I'm sure we can help that girl."

"...Thank you."

Hearing those words made Glenn very happy.

At Tisalia's smile, Glenn felt somewhat embarrassed and shy, and looked away from her.

At that very moment, in front of his averted gaze, a basket was put down with a thud. The inside was packed with a large number of feathers. Glenn glanced up casually and saw that Sapphee was the one who had brought the basket to them. Her eyebrows were twitching slightly.

"Here you are, Doctor. I gathered the feathers."

"Hold on. This is so many, Sapphee... But it looks like there are feathers from other harpies mixed in here with Illy's...?"

"Oh, I didn't realize that. You see, I just happened to catch a glimpse of Dr. Glenn chatting away with the centaur princess, forgetting all about the observations he should be making."

"Hold on, Miss Tisalia was just giving me some encouragement, that's all."

At Glenn's words, the twitching of Sapphee's eyebrows only got worse. For some reason or another, Tisalia gave a loud guffaw.

Glenn wondered if this meant another altercation between

Sapphee and Tisalia was on its way. Quarrels were their chief form of communication with each other, and once they got going, Glenn couldn't help but get wrapped up in trying to mediate the situation.

As Glenn considered how he was going to defuse the situation, Sapphee lowered her eyes. She seemed to have something she wanted to say to Tisalia, but in the end, she simply sighed.

"...Sapphee?"

"It's nothing. I'm going to get back to work."

Sapphee slithered off, hiding her face with her parasol. Normally, this would be the moment when she sent sharp and stinging words Tisalia's way.

The centaur cocked her head to the side in confusion. "...I guess Miss Sapphee must be tired?"

"That can't be."

"She doesn't show it on her face, but a cold wind blows into this village. It might be a hard environment for a lamia to be in... It's important to keep your patients in mind, Doctor, but make sure you show Sapphee some proper appreciation, too—okay?"

"Okay. I'll keep an eye on her."

"Good." Tisalia smiled.

Glenn thought that he was no match for her, after all. Tisalia was fair and straightforward, even when it came to people she didn't see eye-to-eye with, like Sapphee. Glenn couldn't help but respect her honesty and frankness.

"Now then, let's finish this up before the sun goes down." Glenn smacked his cheeks to psych himself up. He was just thinking that he should start by sorting through the feathers Sapphee had brought, when—

A single harpy landed in the village square.

"Dr. Glenn! So, this is where you were!"

It was the man in charge of leading the younger harpies in the village. His muscular body was dazzling, but there was a distinct look of panic on his face.

"What's wrong? Is there an emergency?"

"No...that's not it. Dr. Glenn, have you seen Illy today?"

As they were told this, Glenn and Tisalia looked towards one another. He had a bad feeling about the man's question, but all he could say was, "No, I haven't seen her today."

"It seems Illy isn't anywhere in the village. She's probably left."

Glenn's intuition had proven correct. Next to him, Tisalia pressed her forehead into her hand and let out an exasperated, "That girl...".

"I will look for her," Glenn replied without a second thought. "With her being unable to fly, she shouldn't be able to get far before nightfall!"

Tisalia dashed off before she could hear the last of Glenn's words. She seemed to have some knowledge of where Illy might have gone, though that was most likely not the case. Perhaps Tisalia was thinking to use her naturally strong legs to search every nook and cranny to find her. It was a simple strategy, but with Tisalia's legs, Glenn thought it might not be a bad method to use after all.

Continuing after Tisalia, Glenn also dashed out of the village square. As he left, he thought about the words he wanted to say to Illy when they found her.

The sun was already halfway hidden behind the peaks of the mountains.

✳ ✖ ✖ ✖ ✳

The moon was out.

Illy loved the view of the moon, visible against the cold night. She had heard that the moon that rose over Lindworm was beautiful, but when she finally laid eyes on it for the first time, it had been more splendid than she ever could have imagined. Illy enjoyed staring at it as she flew, or while she sat in the trees or atop a tall building.

Now she could no longer fly.

Nevertheless, Illy still wanted to be someplace high up, as high as she could get. Sneaking away from the village, she clawed her way up a tree using her own strength. Without flight, getting up the tree had given her a hard time. *What an inconvenience*, she thought to herself.

Illy had always lived in the slums. She didn't know her parents. By the time she was old enough to wonder about such things, she was living huddled together with the other children of the slums.

She ate food that she stole from the shops and borrowed roofs without permission to use for her bed. That way of living was common sense to her. She would have been lying if she said it wasn't difficult, but even then, Illy knew that she could survive.

She had powerful wings and sharp talons. She was confident in her ability to win a fight, and if she were ever in a pinch without a way out, she could just escape into the sky. That was how she had regarded her life—at least, until she was plucked up by the slave traders.

"What the hell...?"

Getting captured by the bandits in the first place had been the beginning of her miscalculations.

She was forced to lay countless numbers of eggs. After that, when she thought she would die from her impacted oviduct, that doctor had come to save her. Illy was grateful for that, but shortly after, that overly arrogant and self-important patchwork woman had told her to go to the harpy village. The woman said if Illy didn't have a place to go back to, then she could go there.

But this wasn't the right place for her to live.

Once I see an opening, I'm getting out of this village as fast as possible.

Yet just as Illy began to think this way, her feathers started to fall out. In the beginning, she thought it was the molting that came with the changing of the seasons, just as the doctor had said, but soon she knew that it was definitely something else. She could tell by the way her feathers were falling out. Until now, she had *always* been able to fly when her feathers had come out. That was how she knew it had to be some kind of serious illness.

Illy was sure she could no longer fly.

She had loved flying through the air and was confident she would be able to get through this illness so long as she could fly high into the skies. But now that she was unable to fly, she no longer had any place to go.

She had thought for sure that the doctor who saved her before would be able to do something and had summoned up all her courage to try and meet with him. Despite that, not only had he *not* helped her fly again, but he'd said her condition was nothing more than molting. It had been an utter disappointment.

She *had* been thinking that, even if she couldn't fly, she could at least go to Lindworm and become an arena fighter, but...

"Ugh... Ow..."

Soon after her examination, she had been given a thorough thrashing by Tisalia.

Illy understood now. She knew Tisalia's martial arts were fundamentally different from the style of street fighting that she had picked up in the back alleys of the slums. Illy's unfair and malicious style of fighting wouldn't stand much of a chance against a martial artist whose skills had been learned completely, starting from the fundamentals. She *had* been able to lightly wound her opponent, but it was still a long way off from the clashes in the arena that she admired so much.

"What the hell? Everyone's against me..."

Illy continued to stare at the moon. It held the same commanding presence as always up in the sky. An iridescence shone around it, perhaps because of the slight cloud cover that had formed in the night sky.

Illy thought she was just a joke. No matter what she tried, it all backfired on her. Why couldn't she do *anything*?

She wished she could fly to the moon. What was up there? Was it filled with magnificent wonders, the likes of which were nowhere to be found in a small harpy village like this one? If she had wings, could she fly all the way up there?

In an old legend, there was a rainbow goddess with wings of her own and with them, she raced freely across the sky. Uneducated as she was, Illy only knew a bit of the myth, but she remembered that her name was the same as the goddess from that legend.

You can't go anywhere. Words the centaur had spoken in the middle of their fight echoed in Illy's mind. *High up? Far away? Where are you going to go, flying like that? Someday, the time will come when you have to come down and land. You can't fly forever.*

It was frustrating, but the reason Illy kept thinking back to those words was because she knew that they were true. Even for harpies, extended periods of long-distance flight were exhausting for them. No matter how confident Illy was in her ability to fly, even she had a limit to how far she could go.

Even with her wings—or rather, *because* she had wings—she still had to come back down to earth.

Of course, she knew that she could never go to the moon.

But if I can't go to the moon, where can *I go?* Illy wondered. *Which land can I touch down in?*

✳ ✖ ✖ ✖ ✳

"Doctor, I've found her," Sapphee said.

The sun had set.

Led by Tisalia, Kay, Lorna, and the rest of the young harpies of the village had all been mobilized to look for Illy. Naturally, once day turned to night, it had become difficult to search for her—or at least, that's what they had thought.

"She's around here, on top of the tallest tree in the area. She seems to think she's hidden, but it didn't fool me."

Glenn had forgotten—when it came to seeing at night, Sapphee had no equal, equipped with the ability to sense others' body temperatures. Even without relying on the light of the sun, for a lamia able to "see" body heat, finding a hidden harpy was—if anything—one of her areas of expertise.

Relying on Sapphee's information and confident in the strength of her legs, Tisalia passed through the woods and arrived at the base of the tree Illy was perched in. Glenn safely continued down the mountain path, thanks to both Tisalia's leadership and Sapphee, who slithered along, sticking close to the doctor.

The cedar tree Illy had hidden in was a head taller than those surrounding it. Glenn thought that if one climbed high enough up it, they'd be able to see far down to Lindworm. He had no doubt that the light from the Waterways' glass lamps was quite a beautiful sight to behold.

"No!" Illy shouted. "I won't come down!"

"You're not some kitten stuck in a tree!" Tisalia shouted back. "Accept it!"

"No!"

Up ahead, Glenn could hear voices that sounded like a spoiled child throwing a tantrum and arguing with one of their parents.

Having gotten to the tree first, Tisalia was bickering with Illy, who was still up in the tree. Looking up, Glenn could see Illy clinging to the trunk.

"It's not like I can fly anymore, you know! Just leave me alone!"

"I can't do that," Tisalia said. "Apologize to all of the people you've made worry!"

"Why are you so concerned about me?!"

"Because she wants to butt her head in other people's business," Sapphee whispered, not speaking to anyone in particular. Looking after others and being caring was Tisalia's forte.

In any event, they couldn't just leave Illy to herself.

"Listen to me!" Glenn shouted up to Illy.

Illy was quite high up in the tree. If she lost even a bit of her balance, her inability to fly meant she might end up falling. Glenn wanted to avoid exciting her as much as possible and wait until the other harpies arrived to help them get her down.

"What do you want, you hack?! Did you bring medicine or something?!"

"You don't need any medicine... But it's true, my diagnosis was a little off."

"Huh...?"

"I want you to take a look at this." Glenn took out two different types of feathers from his coat.

Both of them were Illy's feathers. They were almost exactly the same in shape and color. Even if Glenn had looked closely at them, it was doubtful that he would have been able to see the difference between the two.

"Wh-what do feathers have to do with anything?! Wait a second, those are mine! Don't go picking them up without my permission!"

"They were left lying on the ground anyway, right?" Tisalia said.

"It's kinda... kinda embarrassing..." Illy's face grew red at Tisalia's words. Glenn wondered if it had been a bad idea to pick up her feathers without asking her first.

However, it had been the only way Glenn could prove his hypothesis. Besides, Illy definitely wouldn't have given him permission in the first place.

"Let me apologize for taking them without asking," Glenn said. "But, thanks to them, I figured out why your feathers are falling out."

"What?! I don't get what you're trying to say! They both look the same to me!"

"That's right—they're the same feathers." As to be expected of a harpy, who searched for prey on the ground from high in the sky, Illy's eyes were able to get a good look at the two feathers in Glenn's hands even from up in the tree. "These are feathers that grew out of the exact same position on your wing."

"Wh-what does that mean?"

"One of them fell out naturally. The other one was given to me after your fight with Miss Tisalia... They both have a similar shape, so I deduced that they are both the eighth feather of your primary flight feathers."

In other words, her feathers were already growing back in, to some extent. One of them may have fallen out naturally, but the other had been ripped out during her brawl with Tisalia. It wasn't rare for feathers to fall out when one became involved in rigorous physical activity.

"That's why—your feathers will return to normal. Your symptoms are just molting after all."

"What... what does that even matter?!" Illy shouted from up in the tree. Glenn couldn't see from where he was standing, but her voice made it sound like she was crying as she spoke. "Obviously my feathers are going to grow back! Of *course* I'll fly again! What does it matter?! Once I can fly, I'm leaving this village for sure this time! If I can't become a fighter, then there's no other reason for me to stay, is there?!"

"Illy..." Glenn said

He thought her voice sounded miserable and that the shouting was her way of calling out for help. Tisalia stared up at the tree, looking worried, as well.

Illy was in the rebellious stage of her adolescence. Even if that hadn't been the case, Glenn was sure that she wouldn't be reprimanded in the village. Everyone there was nice and would be concerned for her more than anything else, since she had been imprisoned by the slave traders for so long.

No matter who Illy aimed her impassioned rebelliousness at, she wouldn't get any sort of response.

In fact, Glenn thought that Tisalia's method of using her martial arts to get through to Illy might have been close to the best possible answer.

But her rebellious stage was soon to come to an end.

"That's not all." There wasn't a single crack in Glenn's resolve. "While the shape of these two feathers is the same, the color is different. The newer feather has turned red at the base... I'm sorry, Illy. My diagnosis was incorrect after all."

"Huh? So, you're saying..."

"It's true that your symptoms point to molting. However, your molting isn't because your body's preparing for winter. The color of your feathers is going to change drastically from here on out. Slowly but surely, your feathers are shifting to a completely different color. That's because—"

Both Illy and Tisalia held their breath.

"Your wings are molting into those of an adult."

✕ ✕ ✕ ✕ ✕

The moon was out.

Kunai Zenow and her dragon mistress had come and sat in one of the rooms within the Lindworm Central Hospital, the pride of the metropolis of Lindworm. Her mistress sat on the sofa and quietly sipped a cup of tea. Kunai waited directly behind her, standing at attention.

The moon visible from the hospital window was beautiful.

Kunai wondered to herself if this moon were also visible from the harpy village.

"You're worried about Glenn?" a woman asked.

"Yes. Well, we're also worried about Illy, too," Skadi replied.

"That's right, that's right."

Kunai and her mistress were both facing a single woman.

She wore glasses and had a voluptuous body. From the high-quality glasses she wore, it was clear that she earned quite a lot of money working at the hospital. She wore a white coat; Kunai wondered if there was some reason why the woman had purposely left it open around her breasts. Contrary to what one might first suspect, Kunai thought it might have been out of pure carelessness.

The woman was sitting in the hospital director's desk. Her lower body—composed of eight octopus-like tentacles—was meandering around the desk. She was handling the mountain of piled documents. The work seemed to consist only of looking over the documents and signing them. Still, as Kunai watched her line the papers up three and four at a time to complete in one fell swoop, Kunai wondered if her mind was actually capable of keeping up with it all.

It definitely was.

If it hadn't been, Cthulhy Squele certainly wouldn't have been sitting in the director's chair of the city's biggest hospital.

"That's what I mean," Cthulhy said. "You're worried, aren't you Skadi?"

"............" Skadi said.

"That's right. She's a good bodyguard, isn't she? She's praising you, Kunai."

"I'm overjoyed to hear that," Kunai said with a bow.

The voice of her master, Skadi, was extremely quiet. It was

only audible to those people she was extremely close to—such as Kunai Zenow. Cthulhy Squele was another of those select individuals. She was an acquaintance of Skadi's from an age long since passed. As dragons lived to be several hundred years old, the fact that Cthulhy was a close friend of hers meant that Cthulhy had been alive for quite a number of years herself.

The scylla species were monsters with the lower body of an octopus, said to inhabit the deepest parts of the ocean. Known for their long lives, there were records of some of them living for close to eight hundred years. One theory held that they were the descendants of a certain malevolent god, but Cthulhy herself had an extremely serene personality. At least, Kunai had never seen her grow angry before.

Her one fault, however, was her laziness. Indeed, Kunai thought that her tendency to make such unreasonable demands of her protégé was all due to this laziness of hers.

"But you don't need to worry," Cthulhy said. "Illy isn't sick."

"................."

"Huh? 'Why didn't I tell Glenn that?' Well, it'd be boring if I just *told* him, of course. I want my pupil to grow and learn more, after all."

In this manner, the busy duo of Cthulhy and Skadi enjoyed a late-night chat between friends.

Cthulhy was always buried under a mountain of paperwork, while Skadi, sitting opposite her, was the Lindworm City Council representative. She had a mountain of work to do herself. The fact that Kunai was the only bodyguard she had brought along with her to this midnight chat was proof of her mistress's trust in her, and Kunai considered it an honor.

Even so, she was gripped with a feeling similar to envy as she watched Cthulhy speak to her mistress without needing to go through her bodyguard.

"Phoenix." Cthulhy gave Kunai a suggestive glance. "It's a legendary species of monster, also referred to as the immortal bird. It's also said to be a rare species of harpy. Even if its life comes to an end, a phoenix's body becomes wreathed in flame, and it regenerates back to new again. A bird that never dies. An immortal bird with dazzling crimson wings."

Immortal, huh?

Kunai felt a certain resonance in the name of the bird, herself being made up of already dead flesh, patched and stitched together. She thought that though something that was dead and something that didn't die appeared to be complete opposites, they might actually be quite similar.

"But Illy is just a descendent of that species," Cthulhy continued. "Though she may be a blood relative of the phoenixes, the intermingling between different harpy races means that she shouldn't think that she's immortal like the phoenixes of legend. It's just that she will inherit their beautiful crimson feathers, wings that anyone would admire and adore... At the end of the day, Illy herself is nothing more than a normal harpy. Right?"

"................."

"'How did I know?' Of *course* I knew. I'm the hospital director, aren't I?"

Cthulhy Squele.

Without examining the harpy girl even once, simply from hearing of Illy's current condition, she had determined that her feathers falling out meant that she was molting. Not only that, but she had recognized Illy's lineage in an instant—that she had the rare blood of a phoenix in her veins and that her molting was because she was changing from a child into an adult.

When it came to the knowledge of monster biology, one could search the whole continent and not find someone to rival Cthulhy.

"She's being reborn. From drab feathers to wings of fiery crimson." Cthulhy gave her theory as if she were reciting a poem. "That's what an adult phoenix is like. It's hard to believe a child with that lineage was living in the slums and captured by slave traders, though."

"I don't mean to be rude, but..." Kunai cut in, fully aware of her position. Interfering with their conversation was beyond her place as a bodyguard. Feeling relieved that neither of them reprimanded her for her presumptuousness, Kunai continued. "You understood all of that and *still* deliberately sent Glenn up to the village?"

"Well, someone like myself isn't going to attend to a single harpy and her molting, am I? Things here are tough, after all."

She certainly had a lazy attitude to her, but there was an unavoidable element of truth to her words. Working in the metropolis, she examined a hundred monsters every day. Of course, she wasn't the only monster doctor, but Kunai understood just by looking at the massive pile of documents that were currently on her desk that the scope of her responsibilities was immense.

When there was a need for her to take a trip up to the village to examine someone, she could simply leave it up to one of the doctors with less on their plate. Fortunately, among Cthulhy's pupils there was a young doctor with a great deal of promise, the only one she had allowed to open up a practice on their own—Glenn.

"I have a mountain of seriously ill patients I need to attend to. Glenn is capable of dealing with a harpy molting."

"Is that all?"

"That's it. That child... He's got much more time on his hands than I do, you know." Cthulhy stifled her laughter.

Kunai's mistress was laughing as well, behind the veil covering her face. Struggling day in and day out as an influential name in the city, she very rarely got to loosen up like this and laugh. The only exception was when she spoke with Cthulhy.

"Is something wrong, Skadi?" Cthulhy asked.

"............" Skadi said.

"'You dote on your pupil,' you say? Why, of course. He's a very cute pupil. I'll be in trouble if he doesn't gain experience along with Sapphee. How exactly will he diagnosis a phoenix molting, I wonder? There are pop quizzes in the real world, too—just like his time in the Academy."

Cthulhy licked the quill pen she held in her tentacles. The small amount of octopus ink on her tongue transferred to the pen to be used as writing ink. The ink that scylla spit up was very smooth, considered to be of very high quality. Cthulhy used her own and because of it, she never ran out. Thus, using her own ink, she continued signing documents.

"I want him to get more experience quickly and let me take it easy."

While she put her hope in Glenn only so she could neglect her own duties, Cthulhy still used all eight of her legs and continued to work diligently.

Looking up at the moon, Kunai thought that so long as it was Glenn up there, things would surely go well.

As she thought that, she remembered that she had once hated doctors. Even now, she still hated most of them, but she trusted Glenn and didn't hate him at all. The neat, clean stitches that kept her together were his work, after all.

She was supposed to hate doctors, and yet—Kunai suddenly felt embarrassed as such thoughts came into her mind.

Even though no blood ran through her veins, she felt like she had a fever, and her face was growing red.

✳ ✳ ✖ ✳ ✳

"Doctooooor!" Illy's wings flapped wide open. "Doctor! Look at them, look at them! See! See!"

"I've already seen them many times now, Illy."

"Look again! See, look, are there any spots that seem rough, or any places where feathers are falling out? Are they okay?"

"A few of them have fallen out, but they'll all grow back, don't worry." As Glenn gave a nod, Illy laughed mischievously.

She spun around and around in the village square. The wings brought with them a vivid color that one might at first mistake for another harpy's. Every time she laid eyes on Glenn, she would call out for him to stop and check up on the health of her wings.

Illy's wings had taken on a drastic new appearance.

The original red color of her feathers had become an even brighter crimson red and emitted a mysterious power. Her flight feathers had no trace left of their former gray and black colors. With underlying tones of yellow and blue, they further emphasized Illy's beautiful vermillion coloration.

Illy's colors were reminiscent of the cockatoos that inhabited the tropical regions of the world, but the brilliance of her feathers gave the impression that they were ablaze. The hues changed subtly depending on how they reflected in the sunlight. Glenn thought the colors were, perhaps, pretending to flicker like a flame.

Her crest had changed, too. Before, she had only a single feather bobbing up and down atop her head, but now a three-feathered crest had sprung up in its stead, looking like a case of bedhead. Feathers came in and out of sight between the gaps in her hair. That part of her plumage had also changed color to blue and yellow.

Besides those things, nothing else had changed, but the impression she gave was of one who had gone through a drastic transformation.

"Illy!" Catching sight of the harpy from afar, Tisalia's hooves pounded as she raced over. "You're barely wearing anything again! You're a young lady—you need to make sure to dress yourself properly!"

"Whaaat? But then no one would be able to see my feathers!"

"You'll catch a cold like that! And you need to learn some modesty!"

Tisalia's lecturing fell on Illy's deaf ears. The harpy had a bright smile on her face, as if her sulking from before had been nothing more than a lie.

Glenn thought that Tisalia had a point—Illy *was* quite thinly dressed.

He had no doubt that it was to show off the feathers around her neck, but she was wearing a type of outfit that hung by a string to cover up her chest, so her back and the rest of her upper body were entirely visible. With the cold winds of winter beginning to blow, it was an extremely thin layer of clothing. On top of that, considering all the jumping up and down she did, there were parts of her body that were liable to become visible—ones that she definitely shouldn't allow others to see.

Seeing a tender-aged young girl prance around in such an outfit would make anyone, not just Tisalia, want to say something.

"Tee hee hee!"

"Don't laugh when you're being yelled at!"

Glenn was sure that Illy would stay happy no matter what was said to her. Even through Tisalia's lecturing and scolding.

"It's fine! I want everyone to see them!"

"This is quite a different Illy than the one I first examined, isn't it...?" Glenn said. "That reminds me, why exactly were you so guarded when I first came to see you? Did I do something?"

"Huh?! Um...well..." Illy stopped spinning around and

showing off her wings.

"He's right," Tisalia said. "You were so rude to him. Listen, you might have died from your oviduct problem if the doctor hadn't been there, you know. Do you understand?"

"I-I know! It's just...um, that's, you know..." Illy quickly looked down at the ground.

Glenn wondered if he had asked her something invasive but reassured himself that the sudden change in her attitude *was* curious, and he wanted to ask if there were a reason. Illy's face had turned as red as her brand new wings.

"Umm... Well, it's...barrassing..."

"Speak clearly!" Tisalia said.

"Jeez! It's because of my egg laying thing! Dr. Glenn saw all of that! I-I was just embarrassed! That's all!" Illy shouted with her face beet red.

"Oh, well..." Glenn was embarrassed by his own ignorance. Of *course* she would be embarrassed. Although it had been part of a medical examination, he had still helped Illy lay an egg. He had spread her legs open and massaged her stomach, as well. It had obviously been part of a medical treatment, and while that itself wasn't anything for *Glenn* to feel embarrassed about, he could see quite clearly now how it would be embarrassing from Illy's perspective.

"Oh, I gotta go show everyone again! Well, um...bye!" Spinning like a tornado, Illy flew off towards where the other harpies were in the village square. She was clearly running away from Glenn and Tisalia, and he wasn't quick enough to stop her.

Illy's boasting had already become a daily event in the village, and the other harpies looked just a little exasperated as they sang the praises of her wings.

Glenn didn't understand exactly how it worked, but it seemed that certain colors and wing types were a kind of status symbol among harpies. The harpy girls close to Illy's age were completely captivated by her wings, a sight they couldn't see anywhere else.

"She's become totally healthy again, hasn't she?" Sapphee muttered, a hint of amazement and exasperation in her voice.

The rebellious Illy was now just a cheerful young girl. Glenn thought that Sapphee must be thinking about the young mermaid songstress Lulala, whom Sapphee thought of as a younger sister. Illy and Lulala were close in age; Glenn could imagine them getting along quite well if they ever got a chance to meet face to face.

"The village elder was shocked, too," Glenn said. "He couldn't believe she'd change so much just from growing in her adult feathers."

"Yes, indeed."

Phoenix wings. Her origins unknown, Illy's molting had all been part of becoming an adult. It was unlikely that her vivid, flame-like wings were anything other than the wings of the mythic monster, the phoenix. Though, of course, Glenn had never even seen a phoenix himself. All he could do was conclude that the similarity was likely, after reading passages from an old medical text.

"Illy wasn't even aware of it herself, after all."

"How in the world did a descendent of the immortal phoenix end up an orphan in the slums?" Sapphee wondered.

"I'm sure there were a lot of factors that made it end up that way. All we can do is guess, though."

Illy's parents' time—or rather, the period even before that—had been one of many momentous events, including war and its ensuing chaos. Despite all that, the blood of the phoenix had somehow survived down to Illy's generation.

Glenn didn't know what Illy herself thought about it, since she didn't know what her parents looked like—but at the very least, the phoenix wings she was so proud of right now would surely become a form of encouragement as she continued on in life.

"Knowing your heritage is one of the most grounding factors in life. I'm sure her recovery is, in part, because of that knowledge..." *Maybe I shouldn't have done anything at all*, Glenn thought to himself.

After all, her molting would have ended naturally either way—her phoenix wings would grow in without anyone doing a thing. Illy might have recovered all by herself, which meant that there hadn't been any need to examine or treat her in the first place.

"That's not true at all," Sapphee said, immediately cheering Glenn up right as he began to look depressed.

Over in the square, Illy seemed to have found the village elder and was boasting about her wings—but at long last, the village chief ordered her to do some sort of work. She spread her wings, and with two or three powerful flaps, rose up into the air.

A crimson flight.

Her wings weren't just beautiful. They also seemed to excel at flight. There wasn't any extra disturbance in the air as her wings cut through it.

"If she had become an adult while she was still depressed and unprepared, Illy probably would have just gotten confused or grown impudent with her new wings," Sapphee said. "Or she might have actually left the village... I think it's a good thing that you let her know she was probably going to be an adult after it was all over, Doctor."

"R-really?"

"Yes. Though everything beyond that was completely useless." Sapphee was as harsh with her evaluations as ever. This time there were many different areas that Glenn needed to reflect upon.

"Flying away won't do anything." Tisalia was still staring up at Illy as she rose higher. "You can only live where you are. That somewhere you wanted to fly to is exactly where you are now."

While they may have given up their place on the battlefield, Glenn felt the pride of the centaur in Tisalia's words.

There was only one place where Illy could be. Or rather, in some cases, one was unable to choose where one lived. What would Illy do here—and how would she do it? How would she fly from here on out? Glenn thought that Tisalia's way of living would be a good example for Illy to learn from.

A single feather fell to the ground, as if Illy couldn't help but foul the nest she was about to leave. It fluttered down in front of Glenn's eyes.

Instinctively, Glenn reached out and grabbed it.

"...?!"

"Doctor?"

"Oh, u-uh, it's nothing."

It was hot. For a second, it had felt hot, as if it were burning. But, no matter how much he touched it now, the red feather was just a normal harpy feather. There was, of course, no possible way it had actually been on fire.

Was it just my imagination...? Glenn though, wondering if his fatigue had made him feel the nonexistent heat.

On the other hand, what he had felt had been the last vestiges of the continuous death and rebirth of the phoenix, the last heat of their flames. Even as it drifted off into legend, the flame never faded—and now it lived on inside of Illy.

The flame should have cooled long ago, and yet the sense of its scorching heat remained forever on Glenn's fingertips.

That was the feeling he got from her feather.

The Hedonistic Arachne

G LENN'S TRIP TO THE VILLAGE had lasted longer than he originally anticipated.

There were a number of reasons for the extended stay. One was that they were waiting for Kay's sprain to fully heal. Another was that there were more patients he needed to attend to in the harpy village than he had expected. The biggest reason, however, was because of all the earthquakes.

"Ungh," Sapphee said.

"Another one, huh?" Glenn was finishing up some paperwork in the clinic when the desk began to shake.

Ever since Glenn had arrived in the harpy village, earthquakes had come quite frequently. Most of them were only a small shaking, and since Glenn was used to earthquakes, he didn't pay them any mind. Sapphee didn't seem to handle them well at all, though, and would tense up at even the slightest tremble of the earth.

On top of that, larger earthquakes shook the land occasionally, as well. They weren't severe enough to cause damage or injuries in the village, but according to the harpies, the road back to Lindworm had come apart, and some areas were experiencing rock slides, as well.

In other words, they were currently stuck in the village until they could be sure the road down the mountain was safe. As they waited, however, the season grew colder and colder by the day. If the village became blocked off by snow, they'd no longer be able to use the carriage. Glenn's goal was to get out of the village before the snow started to fall.

"Sapphee, you don't have to be so scared."

"There aren't many earthquakes in monster territory," she said in response, as if she were trying to simultaneously show off and make an excuse. "Lindworm gets a fair amount itself, but it's rare to find a monster who isn't scared of them... I'd say it's stranger that you're able to remain so calm, Dr. Glenn."

"Well, my hometown had a lot of earthquakes, so I'm used to them..."

As for the harpies, they didn't seem frightened by the earthquakes, either. *Well*, Glenn thought, *they all have their wings.* They probably figured that if the earth started to tremble, they could just escape into the air.

At that thought, however, Glenn remembered the village elder's frown. It was true that the old harpy had a stern expression to begin with, but he had crinkled his eyebrows even further at the frequency of the earthquakes. After all, being the village leader meant that he couldn't simply relax during situations like this.

"But it *is* strange, isn't it? There are earthquakes almost every day here."

"Honestly," Sapphee said, "I wish they'd give us a break."

"I hope it's not some omen of things to come..." Glenn wasn't startled by the quakes themselves, but he definitely found the frequency of them abnormal.

Fortunately, Kay's sprain had completely healed. Glenn knew that if they could just clear the mountain road, they could be on their way immediately. Tisalia shared his line of thinking.

For now, he just wished the earthquakes would let up a little.

"Dr. Glennnn!" The door flew open with a bang.

Illy dashed into the examination room, her wings as dazzling as ever. With her feathers regrown, she had become completely healthy and energetic—but no matter how one looked at it, she had become a little *too* energetic and was now often scolded by Tisalia and the other harpies in the village.

"Illy! Don't come barging in—stay in the waiting room!" Sapphee yelled.

"What? But—!"

"No buts!" Sapphee yelled at her. Yet, no matter how much she was yelled at, Illy wasn't bothered at all.

Illy had all the energy of a gust of wind; she wouldn't be kept in check from a mere scolding.

"Now, now, Sapphee," Glenn said. "We don't have any patients right now anyway, right?"

"There you go, Doctor! You pick up on things quick!" Illy's crest bobbed up and down. It seemed that she was happy at Glenn's response.

There was a look in Sapphee's eyes that said she still wanted to say something, but in the end she let out a sigh, rubbing the scales at the edge of her eyes. Glenn was sure that it meant he would be lectured again when dinner time came around.

That being the case—

Glenn could already see Illy's reason for barging into the examination room.

"So...what is all this about?"

"If I knew that, I wouldn't have rushed over here!" Every time Illy raised her voice, the crest on top of her head bounced with it. Glenn and Sapphee weren't busy anyway, but that was neither here nor there.

Illy's face down to her chest was covered in something sticky. It was a white, mucus-like liquid. Glenn wondered if she had run through the village looking like this. The unknown substance trickled in thick drops onto the floor of the clinic.

"I was flying through the forest when my head suddenly got caught! Ugh, what *is* this?! Why does this stuff keep happening to me?!"

"Can I touch it?" Glenn asked.

"Uh-huh."

After getting Illy's permission, Glenn touched her cheek.

The mysterious white liquid was stuck to her face from the tip of her nose to her cheek. It clung to Glenn's finger as he touched it.

At first glance, it seemed to be some sort of liquid, but it felt like something different when touched. It was surprisingly hard to free himself from. Less like a liquid... more like a sticky piece of string.

"This feels so gross," Illy said.

"Wait, don't—"

Unable to endure it any longer, Illy started to scrub her face clean with her wings. However, this had the opposite effect of what she intended. The sticky substance, reminiscent of birdlime, stuck to Illy's wings as well. Pulling on the narrow strings made her feathers sticky and tangled.

"Eeeek! It's sticking to me! Doctor!"

"Come on, stop moving. Just stay still."

"Ugh... Got some in my mouth... It's real bitter..."

With her proud wings caught up in the white substance, Illy's face went pale. In the end, the stuff on her face remained. The more she struggled, the more she was held fast by the substance.

Glenn happened to know exactly what it was.

"This is spider silk... No—arachne silk, maybe?" Touching the viscous threads, impossible to free one's hands from, had reminded him.

Arachne were a species of monster who had the lower body of a spider. The characteristic silk they produced was actually used in a variety of different ways. Said to be stronger than steel in the right amount, the silk of the arachne could be spun into clothing if processed properly.

"That's right—your clothes are made from arachne silk, aren't they Sapphee?" he asked.

"That's correct," Sapphee said. "It's quite hard to find anyone who can make light-blocking clothes other than the arachne."

Sapphee's elastic, light-blocking underclothes were the only thing that no other monster species could imitate. Created by arachne who specialized in producing and processing their own silk, it was the finest example of their skill and technique.

Spider silk was quite similar, but arachne didn't produce just one kind of silk. One type was composed of threads spun with an adhesive substance on it used to catch prey. The other was a thread free of adhesive that they could use to hold their own bodies up. Switching between those types of silk at will, they created traps and webs, or made clothes. Their silk truly had a wide range of applications.

As soldiers, arachne were thought to be the strongest military strategists around. That was how capable they were—the arachne used their own silk to deal with any and every problem they might have.

"You must have flown into the trail left behind by an arachne here on the mountain," Glenn said. "It's probably using its webs to get around. How unlucky for you, Illy."

"Grrr. I won't fly so low anymore..."

"That's a good idea. You might end up having another accident." Using their webs to maneuver between the trees was a signature move of the arachne. By flying up above the trees, harpies could avoid getting caught.

"If it's silk from an arachne, then it will come off in hot water. You could even jump in the hot springs to wash it off. I'm sure your clothes will be fine if you wash them there, too.

"Really?! All right then, I'll be off."

With a spin, she began to run off again. She was truly a restless young girl, but Glenn thought this was simply Illy's nature. She just didn't have the personality to sit still inside somewhere.

Illy appeared ready to just sprint straight out of the clinic, but on her way out the door she suddenly stopped. Laughing mischievously, she turned back around.

"Will you come in with me, Doctor? Into the hot springs?"

"Hurry up and get out of here!" Sapphee slapped her tail on the floor with a loud noise. Illy flew out of the clinic after being yelled at, as if she were trying to escape. "Don't be so foolish, Doctor! She's still just a child, you know!"

"I didn't do anything, Sapphee. Calm down."

"How am I supposed to calm down... Rivals keep popping up left and right... Miss Cthulhy and Miss Tisalia are already more than enough of a nuisance as it is!"

Sapphee covered her face and beat her tail against the floor. She had become quite emotionally unstable ever since they'd come to the village. Glenn thought it must be the exhaustion from their work away from Lindworm, coupled with the cold mountain winds of the village, that had made her so insecure.

"Besides..." Sapphee said. "I have a bad feeling. An arachne's silk... It can't be, can it?"

"Do you know something about this, Sapphee?"

"No, I can't say anything yet, but I have a really bad hunch about it..." Rare for her, Sapphee showed her own unrest clearly in her expression.

Considering how smart and attentive to detail Sapphee was, her bad hunch had a fairly high chance of proving to be true.

"We have to pull ourselves together, then. Right, Sapphee?"

At Glenn's words, Sapphee kept her face covered and gave a slight nod of her head.

✖ ✖ ✖ ✖ ✖

Over the next few days, there was a sharp increase in the number of harpies that came into the clinic.

Most of those who came were like Illy—they'd been flying through the forest, then got stuck in arachne webs when taking off or landing. The silk could be washed off with hot water, but it seemed that the harpies in the village hadn't come into contact with arachne webs before and came to the clinic because it felt creepy and gross.

The ones who were harmed the most were the young harpies who went out patrolling to make sure the mountain road was safe.

"Huh. This is...a problem," Glenn said.

"Yes, quite a problem," Sapphee agreed. Her intuition had been right on the mark.

If the harpies' wings got even the slightest bit entangled in the webs, they were completely unable to fly. Their wings required a certain degree of subtle, fine operation to work. The young harpies had been clearing the mountain road of any danger, as well as checking the way down to Lindworm for Glenn and the others' return to the city, but that work was now delayed by the mysterious arachne webs.

It was also easy to think that if a harpy became entangled in a strange position when they were taking off or landing, their struggling in the webs might cause them to drop down to the ground. Fortunately, there hadn't been anyone injured by such a fall, but with the number of people coming in everyday because of the spider webs, it was only a matter of time until a serious injury occurred.

For this reason, Glenn began to wonder: *What should we do?*

First, he asked for the village elder's help and told everyone in the village how to deal with the arachne silk. There wasn't any fundamental difference between what he said to the harpies at large and what he had first told Illy. If they washed themselves in the hot springs, all of the sticky silk would wash away. They didn't need to come all the way to the clinic for Glenn's help.

On the other hand, the threat that the silk posed needed to be taken care of.

Thinking it would be much faster to go himself, Glenn went into the mountain forest. He was confident he could trace the webs and thus track the arachne who spun them. Glenn didn't know why the arachne was on the mountain, but no matter what the reason, he just wanted them to stop stretching out their webs everywhere so indiscriminately.

It wasn't an unreasonable request, so Glenn was confident the arachne would listen to what he had to say. The problem was whether or not he would be able to find the arachne in the vast mountain forest.

"You didn't have to come with me, you know, Sapphee."

"Not at all. It's possible this might actually be someone I'm acquainted with."

Sapphee wore a sun-blocking veil that covered her face. Considering her albinism, Glenn couldn't help but worry whenever she left the clinic during the day. On the other hand, it was nice having a lamia accompany him through the forest. Lamia had originated in hot, humid tropical forests. They could move easily through the tangled brush with their lower bodies, and they weren't affected by the variations in elevation. At the slightest difference in steepness, Sapphee would carry him up in her tail, which helped Glenn greatly as he hiked.

It was easy to imagine an inexperienced hiker becoming lost on a mountain they weren't familiar with, but Glenn had taken measures to deal with that as well. In the sky overhead, Illy frequently circled with her colorful wings. The plan was that if Sapphee and Glenn became lost in the forest, she would fly down and guide them. They had also asked her to let them know if she happened to spy someone that resembled the arachne they were looking for.

Illy's expression of pride and triumph at being called upon for help had left an impression on Glenn.

Thus, the three of them—Glenn, Sapphee, and Illy up high in the sky—formed a three-person team intent on tracking down the arachne.

Glenn didn't know why the mysterious arachne weighed so heavily on Sapphee's mind, but he was sure she had her reasons.

As they went further into the mountain forest, the entire area became thick with webs. Glenn suspected that these weren't webs to capture prey, but instead those arachne used to get around with ease. He had heard there were also some arachne who spun their silk to the branches of the trees, swinging and jumping like a pendulum again and again to travel long distances.

"Be careful, Doctor," Sapphee said. "Arachne are skilled at laying traps."

"I'm sure we won't fall into any traps, right?"

"I wonder."

Stepping and slithering firmly against the earth, they continued further into the mountain forest.

It wasn't hard to track the arachne. The trail of webs told them the specific direction in which the mysterious arachne was moving.

"At any rate," Sapphee said, "the arachne I know well is...a little odd." She seemed to be talking to herself, but Glenn could hear a warning in her voice.

"It'll be fine. There's no way I'll be caught in a web that's visible to the naked eye like these are."

✖ ✖ ✖ ✖ ✖

Glenn regretted his own words a few short minutes after saying them.

"I *told* you to be careful," Sapphee said.

"I'm ashamed..." Glenn said with a groan.

Unaware of an arachne web placed at his feet, Glenn had fallen down. It seemed that the web he'd fallen on had some sort of pressure-sensitive function and a thread that extended down from the treetops to Glenn on the ground. It lifted him up where he lay with both of his hands tied cleanly behind his back.

Unable to move in the entangled web, it was as if Glenn were a condemned criminal being hung. Indeed, if there had been a string of silk caught around his neck, it would have been more than a metaphor—he really *would* have ended up as a corpse.

The trap had been laid out quite cleverly, the web stuck to blades of grass and camouflaged so it wouldn't be noticeable at a glance. Once one was caught by it, it chained together into the next trap and semi-automatically crucified the arachne's prey to the tree. It seemed that the arachne who had made the trap was outrageously skilled.

The web Glenn had fallen prey to was clearly different from all the webs they had seen earlier. It was obviously a trap made to capture any human that stepped further beyond where they were.

"Sapphee, I'm sorry, but do you think you can untangle me?"

"How about you stay like that for a little while? It's a good lesson for someone so careless."

"Come on, don't be spiteful..."

Glenn couldn't do anything while he remained trapped, unable to move, but it seemed that Sapphee had no intentions of helping him down.

"Unfortunately, if I touch an arachne's silk, I'll end up getting tangled in it as well. I very much want to help you, but...please just bear with it for a while."

"Ugh..."

Sapphee wasn't being cold, however, but instead plotting a precise method with which to get him down.

However, Glenn's bound hands would soon start hurting, which made sense, considering the unnatural pose his body was twisted into. If he weren't able to get free of the silk, it was possible his body might suffer ramifications from the experience later on.

"Well, whatever the case, it's no problem," Sapphee said.

"It definitely is a problem. It's painful being kept in a pose like this."

"The news that a scatterbrain has gotten caught in a trap will travel to the one who laid it through the threads of silk... I'm sure it won't be long before they come to get a look at said scatterbrain's face."

"Come here?" *Who was coming?* Glenn thought.

The answer was obvious, of course: the arachne that had spread out the trap.

✖ ✖ ✖ ✖ ✖

"Oh dear. My, my, my." The voice was coming from up above.

A black shadow covered Glenn, as if it had blocked out the sun filtering down through the treetops. The voice had a refreshing tone to it, but at the same time spoke with a leisurely drawl.

"Ah, if it isn't Sapphee. I wondered who that might be. Long time no see, dear."

"So, it was you, after all...Arahnia," Sapphee said.

"Oh, no—why, what a frightening face you're making. You should be happy to see me." With nimble movements unsuitable for its enormous body, the shadow descended from the trees.

It was an arachne with beautiful, straight black hair.

Arachne had a total of twelve arms and legs. They had four arms on their human-like upper body; on their lower body they had eight legs like a spider.

With her four human arms, the arachne standing before Glenn cleanly pulled in her threads and approached him quickly.

"Now, what ever could you be up to on a little old mountain like this?" she asked.

"We're in the middle of a trip to the harpy village to treat patients there," Sapphee replied. "A better question would be what are *you* doing here, Arahnia?"

"Well, I heard a little rumor, you see... Oh, is that it? This careless gentleman here must be the doctor you're always talking about."

The woman got even closer to Glenn. She had deep red eyes beneath her evenly cut black hair. All eight of her spider legs moved as if they were each their own separate organism, letting her make agile movements that didn't appear possible with her large body.

"Greetings, Doctor. I am Saphentite's close friend—Arahnia Taranterra Arachnida. It's quite a pleasure to meet you."

"Close friend?" Glenn glanced over to Sapphee and she gave a slightly defeated nod of her head.

At Arahnia's words, Glenn actually got the feeling that he could see similarities between her and Sapphee. Her calm expression and manner, her long hair, and the indescribable source of fear bubbling underneath the surface. For Sapphee, this fear came from being descended from assassins—but where did it come from for Arahnia?

Her clothes were bizarre. She wore what looked like a party dress, her large breasts pulling it open. On the other hand, she also wore an obi around her middle, much like those worn with the kimono that were seen in the eastern edge of the humans' territory. The alternating black and white pattern of her dress was one that Glenn couldn't remember ever seeing before. She seemed to be a woman who was fond of fine, fashionable clothing.

On her upper body, she had a pair of arms that extended from her shoulders, much like a human's, as well as another pair situated beneath the first. The second pair looked the same as the arms of a human but were in fact equivalent to the pedipalps of a spider.

On each of her hands, she had long nails that had been painted and manicured. The color of her manicured nails was also quite mysterious. They were a strong, reddish pink, a depth of color that wasn't a simple hue of red. Glenn couldn't imagine what kind of dye would produce such a color.

"She's a designer," Sapphee said.

"Designer?"

"That's right. She's the dressmaker for the Lindworm branch of Loose Silk Sewing. My nurse's outfit, and the outfit she is wearing now, are all her own personal designs."

Glenn was amazed. Loose Silk Sewing was a famous company that had shops all across the continent. The entire company was comprised solely of arachne, and they mainly produced and sold clothes for monsters. Clothes made from the threads of the arachne were famous for being even higher quality than regular silk. They handled a variety of different fashions, each adapted to various different species of monsters.

Arahnia was a dress designer for such a large company. She looked young, but held an important title in a sizeable business. It seemed that she was a youthful, but quite capable, individual.

"I'm Glenn Litbeit. Nice to meet you..." It felt somewhat odd for him to be greeting someone for the first time while tied up against a tree.

Yet Arahnia didn't seem to find it odd at all. She smiled at him and said, "Yes, yes, I've heard about you. Despite appearances, Sapphee is a drinking buddy of mine. She often tells me about you when we're together."

"I became familiar with Arahnia after I began ordering clothes from her," Sapphee said. "She can be a little difficult at times, but she's hardworking and friendly woman."

It seemed that, unbeknownst to Glenn, Sapphee had also been making more friends throughout the city. Now that he thought about it, she often went out at night, saying she was going drinking with a friend. Since it was unlikely for Sapphee to get drunk to the point where she was falling down, Glenn had never been very worried. It seemed that Arahnia was the one she had been meeting up with all those times.

Though Arahnia had said they were close friends, there was a sharp look in Sapphee's eyes as she stared at Arahnia, as if she were on her guard for some reason.

"So, then...why are you here, Miss Arahnia?" Sapphee asked.

"Well, you see..." Arahnia flicked her long nail and pointed it towards Glenn.

Arahnia's hand had five porcelain white fingers and was very beautiful. She used those five fingers and her legs to manipulate thread with ease. Much like spider webs were sometimes patterned like works of art, the threadwork of the arachne crossed over into the domain of art, as well.

Arachne had indeed reached the absolute peak of silk making.

"I've heard that there is a harpy with phoenix wings here on the mountain."

"Y-you're quick on the uptake," Sapphee said.

Glenn knew immediately that she was talking about Illy. The only thing she had inherited from her phoenix lineage was the pattern of her wings—but that wasn't necessarily the point.

"Don't underestimate the information network of the arachne. We've spread our web across the whole continent, you know... How wonderful, though! A phoenix! I wanted today to be the day I'd capture that miraculous figure with the beautiful seven-colored wings, able to change hue freely with only a flap."

"I think you're exaggerating a bit..." Glenn said.

"I'm sure wings of such beauty will give me inspiration for my latest work!"

Glenn figured it out. At last, he understood what Arahnia's goal was.

Looking closely at her, she had a number of pouches tied to her spider legs. In them, he could see glimpses of paint brushes and charcoal. In other words, she was intending to sketch the young phoenix girl that had appeared in the village and would afterward use her drawings as a reference for the new clothes she was going to make.

Glenn thought that it was just as Sapphee had said—Arahnia seemed to take her work very seriously.

"Well, I must admit that I never expected Dr. Glenn to get caught in the trap I made to capture the phoenix... Forgive me, okay? I'll untie you now."

"Y-you were going to capture her with a trap?!" Glenn said.

"Hm? How else would you have me do it, then?" Arahnia tilted her head as if she truly didn't understand what Glenn was saying. "I wouldn't be out here in the mountains camping and spreading traps everywhere if I weren't trying to catch the phoenix..."

"Wait a second, Miss Arahnia. You didn't actually think the phoenix was a wild harpy, did you?"

"Huuuh?" She had a completely serious look on her face, but Glenn wondered if she was just playing innocent.

No, he decided after a moment, that didn't seem to be the case. She had an artsy air about her, but it seemed she was a bit of an oblivious airhead, as well.

"The girl you're looking for is living in the village, you know. She's a completely integrated member of the community."

"Y-you must be joking with me, right?"

Glenn now understood why the harpies of the village had been getting caught in her threads. Arahnia had been going all around the woods, continuously spreading traps for Illy. Since her hunting grounds were slightly off from the harpies' area of activity, she hadn't yet captured any harpies. However, because of that, Arahnia's misunderstanding had never been corrected.

"You should have just come to the village first," Sapphee said. "You're always doing things in a little off-kilter manner like this."

"Well, I wish you would have told me that sooner..." Arahnia used her four arms to hold her head in her hands.

At that moment, a trivial thought popped into Glenn's head: maybe the more arms one had, the more troubles and worries one had to hold with them.

✕ ✕ ✖ ✕ ✕

Having spent her whole time on the mountain camping, Arahnia was happy to sleep under a roof for the first time in a long while. The drive it had taken for her to dare to camp out in the mountains just to get a glimpse of the phoenix was, perhaps, admirable, but...it had brought with it the recklessness of not properly considering what came ahead of her.

In any event, Glenn thought she certainly had an uncommon passion and zeal for her work.

At a glance, she had the air of a composed, dignified young lady. Combined with her leisurely accented drawl, Arahnia gave a modest, soothing impression. Yet...

"Hmph."

In the middle of their conversation with the village elder, Arahnia twisted her head around as a hurried red wind passed behind her.

Arahnia had six eyes in total—though at first glance, she seemed to only have two eyes, much like a human. In reality, however, she had four small compound eyes on her forehead. It was said that an arachne's vision wasn't very good, but it seemed that her eyes were sharp enough to take notice of the harpy with lustrous wings loitering about the village.

"That must be the phoenix from the rumors! Hey, young lady—I have to speak with you! Show me those wings of yours!"

"Eh?!" Illy said. "What the—a spider?! Wait, who are you?!"

"Who I am is but a trifling matter! Don't you worry about that—just show me those wings!"

"No, wait—stay away!"

"I just want to see your wings! Just a little, even the tips would be fine!"

"No way!" Illy made to escape using her natural agility, but Arahnia wouldn't be beaten.

Arachne had no bones in their lower body. Instead, they had a light and sturdy exoskeleton, which allowed them to move spryly despite their large size. Despite the harpy's fleetness of foot, Arahnia chased after Illy.

"I won't even ask for a sketch. Just give me one feather!"

"Noooooo! Get away from me!"

"Please! I promise I won't ask for anything more!"

"Gyaaaaaaaah!"

For a while, the two of them chased each other around the village square before finally running out of sight. Glenn scratched his head, troubled, hoping that Illy didn't wander off to the mountain as she ran away.

With a pale look on her face, Sapphee apologized to the village elder over and over again. He didn't seem to mind at all, though it was clear that Arahnia's hardworking behavior had a sort of frightening edge to it.

"They won't be back for a while," Sapphee said with an exasperated tone to her voice.

To Glenn, it seemed that, though she sounded amazed at Arahnia's behavior, she seemed happy, as well. While she didn't grow loud and talk cheerfully with her, Sapphee had seemed to be enjoying her conversation with Arahnia.

Arahnia *had* said she was a close friend. The city of Lindworm had always been a city totally comprised of foreigners and outsiders. The harpies on the mountain had lived in the region since long ago, while the City Council representative Skadi, and Glenn's teacher Cthulhy, had both come from distant lands. Glenn, Sapphee, and even Tisalia were the same.

However, just because the city was full of people from a variety of backgrounds and origins didn't mean it was easy to quickly make friends. Glenn thought that Arahnia must have been one of the few friends Sapphee had been able to make in a city full of strangers and foreigners like Lindworm.

"Dr. Glenn." Sapphee's conversation with the village elder appeared to be over, and she turned now to face the Doctor. "For now, Arahnia will stay in the village. We've been given the elder's permission, as well. It's up to Arahnia herself how long she wants to stay, but I'm sure she'll return to Lindworm once she gets her fill of looking at Illy."

Glenn wondered if she'd really be able to get enough of a look at Illy to be satisfied. After all, Illy didn't seem keen on the arachne's attention, running away as she was. If things continued like this, he couldn't imagine that Arahnia would be able to get enough information to use as a reference for her dresses.

"Also, we've gotten her promise that she won't put her silk all over the mountain. That way, fewer harpies should fall victim to Arahnia's threads."

"What was that you said?!" A large body crept into view from behind Sapphee.

"You're saying there'll be fewer victims, huh?! A fine thing to say. Look at me! Look at what's happened to me! Thanks to an encounter with that street-slasher spider woman, I've been covered in silk! Auuuggggh, what am I going to do?!" It was Tisalia Scythia.

From her face down to her breasts, she was covered with sticky white threads of arachne silk. The dripping white substance was all over Tisalia's well-developed breasts. She was in a horrible state. Tisalia wiped her face to try and get it off, but that only had the opposite effect, entangling her hand, as well.

"Oh, how unlucky," Glenn said.

"This doesn't have anything to do with luck! That spider-woman gave a 'pardon me' as she chased Illy right past me! Sending her threads flying to move is tolerable enough, but it's being caught in all of it that I can't stand! What in the world is up with her?!"

"She's my friend," Sapphee said.

"You need to choose your friends better!"

It seemed that Tisalia had been taking a walk somewhere or another, encountered Arahnia, and in a bad string of luck had arachne silk poured over her—or at least, that's what Glenn could surmise from the situation.

"All over one of my favorite outfits, too..."

"If you dip it in hot water, it will come out," Glenn said.

"Leaving such a dangerous woman to scamper about as she pleases! Honestly, what is the meaning of this?!"

Glenn was taken aback a moment.

From what Glenn knew about Tisalia, she never spoke poorly of others. While she sang her own praises and was proud, she didn't often show contempt for others. *Well,* Glenn thought, *Sapphee being the one exception.*

Glenn wondered if Tisalia actually disliked Arahnia just as much as she did Sapphee, despite the fact that—as far as Glenn was aware—they hadn't ever met? Was Tisalia really capable of detesting someone before she got to know them?

Sapphee gave a slight shrug of her shoulders. Glenn was sure that she wouldn't be pleased to hear someone speak ill of the woman whom she referred to as her close friend.

"It is true that it's in her character to sometimes lose track of her surroundings, but Arahnia isn't a bad person. Please don't say she's dangerous or anything like that," Sapphee said.

"Oh, well *this* is a rare moment for the wise Miss Sapphee. You can tell at a glance how dangerous she is! I mean really—you're her friend, but you still haven't noticed?"

"I assume, then, it's fair to consider that remark as your own prejudice against the arachne?"

"That's not it! That's not what I meant." Tisalia shook her head. "Those types are moody."

"Your point being? It's true, she is moody, but the way she works when she's let herself loose into one of her moods is splendid. My clothes were also her design."

"Those types of people, you know, they can't be trusted. She—Miss Arahnia, was it? She covered me in her silk, yet she didn't show any sort of remorse. That's the face of an evil woman."

Glenn wondered if this was what was known as a woman's intuition.

Tisalia seemed unusually on edge. Even the ears on top her head were perked straight up, which told Glenn she was on high alert.

"It's okay, Miss Tisalia," Glenn said, thinking that if he didn't come in as the peacemaker, their fighting wouldn't stop. "It seems that Miss Arahnia just wants to see Illy's wings, to use as a reference to design a new dress. That's all."

"Is that really all it is, though? I wonder if she's scheming up something or other."

"Something like what?"

"Well...! I don't really know."

"In that case, I'm sure you're worked up over nothing."

Tisalia still seemed unconvinced.

Glenn wondered what it was that made her so wary of Arahnia. She was an eccentric woman, but all of the monsters he knew were a little eccentric in their own ways... He couldn't quite explain it, but it wasn't like Tisalia to get so upset just from being exposed to some of Arahnia's silk.

"I'll make sure to tell my friend you said that," Sapphee said.

"Did I offend you? It's just, I—"

"No, if that's what you're saying, you should just stick with it, right? That's more like you, anyway." Now Sapphee was acting somewhat strange as well.

Her words were also very unusual for her. Was she cheering Tisalia on? Protecting her? Glenn got these impressions from her words, but on the other hand, it also felt as if she was somehow forsaking Tisalia.

Glenn thought that everyone was acting weird. Ever since Arahnia arrived, an odd tension had been hanging in the air among the womenfolk.

"Arahnia is here, yes," Sapphee said. "But we've got a strong person like Miss Tisalia here in the village right now, so even if she's scheming up something, it'll be fine, right?"

"Are you perhaps...being sarcastic?" Tisalia asked.

"Hmm, I wonder?"

Almost as if announcing their conversation was over, Sapphee slithered away in the direction of the clinic.

Left behind, Tisalia let out a sigh. "She's definitely feeling tired."

"Huh?" Glenn said.

"Perhaps it's because of the cold here in the village. Doctor, please give her your support."

Glenn was at a loss. He hadn't seen Sapphee looking fatigued at all, and she had been as precise with her work as ever. He knew it was true that as a species they were weak to the cold, but...

"She's trying too hard," Tisalia said. "It's because she wants to do her best for the doctor she loves so much."

"I hadn't noticed it at all..."

Tisalia had pointed out Sapphee's condition to Glenn before, but he had ultimately ended up ignoring it.

Sapphee hadn't let it show on her face—not even when she was pushing herself to the limits. That was the type of personality she had. Generally, her tail expressed her emotions more eloquently than her facial expressions did.

"I suppose even a great physician can be slow to discern the condition of those closest to him?" Tisalia said.

"I don't have anything I can say to that..."

Sapphee had always been a capable person. Without realizing it, Glenn had started relying on her too heavily. On top of that, she was older than him and had always been like an older sister to him. Perhaps he had been taking advantage of her somewhat.

Believing Tisalia's words to be true, Glenn decided to let Sapphee relax a bit. Their long stay in the village might have put more of a burden on Sapphee than he had thought.

"I'm going to go wash this silk off." With those words, Tisalia left Glenn as well.

"Oh, uh, okay."

Both Tisalia and Sapphee seemed to have something on their minds, but the subtleties of the two women were beyond him. He could pick out the focus of an infection but was still far too young a man to pick out the inner workings of a woman's heart.

✖ ✖ ✖ ✖ ✖

Ultimately, Glenn did have Sapphee take a break from her work.

The number of victims of Arahnia's webs had decreased and work at the clinic had calmed down. He told her that he wanted her to take a nice long soak in the hot springs to make herself feel better again and that now was a good opportunity to do so.

"I feel fine," Sapphee said.

"Take a break anyway. I've been having you work too hard lately... I want you to relax a little. Think of it as a present from me."

"A present...from Dr. Glenn... In that case, I'll do as you wish."

After that conversation, Sapphee had consented to taking some time off.

For several days, Glenn would manage the clinic by himself. With fewer patients coming in and the helper fairies on hand, he would be able to manage perfectly fine even on his own.

Sapphee is likely soaking in the hot springs right now, Glenn thought to himself as he worked.

Kay and Lorna had been worried for Sapphee and took her there themselves. They may have been acting on secret orders from their mistress, but whatever the case, Glenn was sure that, at that moment, the three of them were enjoying themselves in the warm waters.

Poikilothermic species of monster were weak to changes in temperature, particularly the cold. The cold was quite draining on a lamia's strength and they didn't hibernate in the winter like snakes. Glenn figured it would be good if Sapphee could get even a little bit more energy from the warmth of the hot springs.

However.

Glenn still hoped that any patients planning on coming to the clinic would wait until Sapphee returned, but—

"What, is Sapphee not here?" It was Arahnia, coming to visit the clinic.

Skillfully folding up her eight legs, she had somehow managed to fit herself inside the tiny clinic.

As aforementioned, arachne were a race of monsters with a spider-like lower body. The large spider abdomen that bulged out behind them and the eight spider legs that stretched out on either side made arachne look giant compared to the actual measurements of their body's length. For all that, the surprisingly spry and skillful way they could move their bodies was a special ability of their race.

Glenn shouldn't have felt any need to be intimidated by Arahnia, but nevertheless found himself shrinking back from her presence.

"I'm sorry, I've had Sapphee take a break. She won't be working here in the clinic for a few days."

"Oh, is that so, then? That certainly is a pity, but I suppose nothing can be done about it." She spoke in the official language of the continent, but she had a strongly pronounced accent that came from the eastern part of the humans' territory. Long ago, many arachne lived in the humans' territory and were sometimes referred to as "jorougumo" in the language of the humans of the east. That word, however, came with a considerably discriminatory connotation.

If she *were* from the east, maybe she was from the same province as he. He wondered if the uniqueness of her outfit's radical design was a result of her incorporating elements of eastern culture.

"Is something bothering you today?" Glenn asked, giving his standard greeting while thinking offhandedly that he had nothing to talk about with her. Sapphee was the one who was friends with Arahnia, after all. The first time he had ever met her had been the day they met on the mountain. Glenn didn't know what he should say to her, or do, except give her an exam like he did all his patients—and yet...

When he thought back to Tisalia and Sapphee's exchange, he felt slightly on guard, despite the fact that Arahnia was completely faultless in the whole affair.

"Well, my head's been feeling a little hazy, you see," she said. "And I've got a bit of an ache in my joints." Arahnia shifted the joints of her lower body. Each time her legs moved, her exoskeleton rubbed against itself, producing a grating, stiff noise.

Despite saying her head was hazy, she didn't *look* very sick—not judging by her face, at least. Glenn wondered if it were simply in her nature to keep her sickness from showing on her face.

"Hm... In that case, could you let me take your temperature for a moment?" he asked.

"Why, certainly. Go right ahead."

Pulling back her evenly cut bangs, Arahnia's covered up forehead was thus exposed. The four small compound eyes there looked like four red rubies.

Glenn placed his hand on her forehead, covering up her compound eyes.

"...You don't seem to have any fever."

"So it seems, doesn't it?"

"Now, then—this time will you open your mouth for me?"

"Aaaah." Arahnia opened up her mouth, and Glenn got a glimpse of her bright red tongue. Her fang-like teeth were impressive.

Pushing her tongue down with a disinfected tongue depressor, Glenn examined the inner part of her throat, but could find no irritation or inflammation.

"Your throat looks fine, too."

"Ahfh ouhu duhaun?"

"Oh, excuse me. I'm finished."

Glenn couldn't find any symptoms that stood out to him, but that didn't mean he could ignore the complaints of a patient.

"I didn't see any problems during my examination," he said. "It may just be the beginnings of a cold. The mountain air might have something to do with it. Have you been having headaches?"

"Why, yes I have. Both my head and throat have been hurting."

Sounds like it's a cold, Glenn concluded.

As he wrote down her symptoms on his charts, he thought to himself that, considering her symptoms, she would heal with a little bit of bed rest. Giving her any medicine would just be an unnecessary cost for her, so for now it wasn't necessary. He could give her a prescription for something if her symptoms grew worse in the coming days.

Despite her cold-like symptoms, Arahnia smiled and observed Glenn as he worked.

"...Is there something else you were curious about?" he asked.

"No, not at all. I was just thinking to myself, 'Wow, a human doctor really is examining monster patients, isn't he?' That's all."

"That's right. I give my patients the utmost care."

"I've been asking myself what sort of person this 'Doctor' that Sapphee always talks about was, but now I see. So, you're the one Sapphee's set her eyes on, huh."

Hearing this made Glenn embarrassed. He was very much aware of Sapphee's affection for him. However, at the moment, not only was he so consumed with running the clinic that he had little time to spare for love, Cthulhy would be enraged if they became occupied with lovers' talk. Glenn wanted to avoid that as much as possible.

For now, he wanted to do his best to avoid breaking their doctor and assistant relationship. It was a dividing line that was necessary for Glenn to continue being a doctor of monster medicine.

"Were you able to get a look at Illy's feathers?" he asked.

"Why yes, I was. I even managed to get a sketch. I have to return to Lindworm as soon as possible and finish my design, but... it seems that the road back is filled with rocks and debris again. It's put me in quite the bind."

"The mountain road *would* be rough while you have this cold of yours. I would say you should take it a little bit easier before trying to go back."

"If I relax too much, the snow will start falling." Arahnia gave a cackling laugh. There were very few women in Lindworm with a laugh like hers. She let out a moan as she stretched out her arms and arched her back. "But you're right, I'll wait until this cold is gone. I suppose I'll go out and take in some of the fresh air?"

"It's not good for your cold to expose yourself to the wind."

"I'm sure just a little is fine, right? Oh, Doctor." Arahnia's red eyes pierced through Glenn as she gave him a fleeting glance. Even with her hair covering some of them, she *did* have a total of six eyes on her head. Simply put, her sight was three times better than a human's. "If at all possible," she said, "would you join me for a walk?"

× × ✖ × ×

Glenn had a number of reasons for going along with Arahnia's invitation.

First was that the clinic was not busy. Although he had to be ready for any emergency that might come his way, it was still good to get a change of atmosphere now and then. He figured it would be no problem for him to take a walk through the village. In fact, it was possible he was feeling exhausted without even knowing it and in need of a break.

The other reason was that he was worried about Arahnia. Although she was only experiencing cold-like symptoms, he couldn't neglect someone who was sick. Furthermore, she was a guest in the village, and she didn't have any close acquaintances there besides Sapphee. He was confident that just accompanying her on her walk would make her feel at ease.

However, Glenn was beginning to think that he had been mistaken in his judgement.

"Miss Arahnia."

"What is it?"

"How far are you planning on going?"

Glenn had accompanied Arahnia through the village, but now they were on the outskirts and there were no trace of the harpies. If they kept going, they would be well on the path leading to the mountain's summit. A cold wind raged through the heights of the Vivre Mountains—the same one that brought the sharp chill to the air in the harpy village.

In short, it was not a path one set out to climb when one just wanted to take a short stroll.

"I wonder... I suppose wherever the mood takes me?" she replied.

"...Why don't we head back soon? This will only make your cold worse."

"Now, now, Doctor, just a little further." Arahnia continued down the path, moving her spider legs with a chittering irregularity.

It was strange. Glenn had thought she'd come to the clinic because she was feeling sick. However, right now she didn't look sick at all—in fact, she seemed much livelier and more active than she had back there.

The path continued deep into the mountains.

Without Glenn noticing, Arahnia had taken out the shears she used for cutting cloth. Just as Glenn was wondering what they were for, Arahnia started to use them to cut off the flowers that were growing on the side of the path and place them in the pouches tied to her spider legs. Glenn wondered if this was also to use as a reference for her designs.

This isn't good, Glenn thought. They were marching completely into the middle of the mountains.

Glenn was wearing what he always did—his tunic and the white coat he wore over top. He was obviously not prepared for a walk through the mountains. Naturally, he thought the same should have been true for Arahnia, but...

"Miss Arahnia?"

"Hmm?"

This time she was distracted by a butterfly fluttering nearby. She didn't appear to be listening to Glenn's words at all.

"I'm going to start heading back."

He didn't wait for an answer and put his back to Arahnia. For just an instant, he hesitated at the thought of leaving Arahnia behind. But when he gave it some more thought, he had to remind himself that she was a bold woman—she had climbed the mountain by herself and set up camp for a number of days, after all.

It seemed to him that she should have decided to go back much sooner.

Right as he took a step back towards the village—

"Watch," came Arahnia's curt reply, "your step." They weren't words of caution; they were a declaration of victory.

There were threads of silk spread out in front of him; they took Glenn off his feet. He thought his face would crash hard into the ground, but the threads flying out all around held his body up. He remembered this sensation. It was just the same as before, an arachne-made trap.

As Glenn spoke out in alarm, he was suspended in midair.

"Ngh?!"

"See, that's why I told you to watch your step."

"Since when were you making a trap?!"

"From the start. It didn't catch you on the way, but I laid it out so it would capture you when you went to try and return to the village. How does it go, again? 'Going is easy, but the return is...'" Arahnia brought up an old eastern children's song to tease Glenn.

Arahnia had already spread her threads over the mountain path. She was now crossing her four arms back and forth, creating a kind of cat's cradle or something similar, but her manipulation of the threads of silk was too fast for Glenn's eyes to follow.

"This time the trap is a serious one. If we arachne feel like it, we can make traps that are imperceptible to the human eye, after all."

"Why did you...? So then, you saying you were feeling sick was...!"

"A. Lie. Tee hee hee hee."

Glenn could feel nothing but a sense of dread from Arahnia's smile of satisfaction.

Back before humans and monsters fought against each other, each monster species lived as they saw fit with other members of their species. Centaurs lived on the grassy plains, lamia lived in the forests, mermaids lived in the rivers and seas—and Arachne lurked on the roadways.

In other words, they lurked on the routes traversed by humans and other species of monsters. The arachne would lay traps there and subsist on the bodily fluids of their prey. Some subspecies of arachne would suck blood. When their prey was a human male, though, they would sometimes drain their fluids through forced sexual intercourse. The all-female arachne race attacked other races in this way, made children when the time came, and thus grew their territory.

Their custom of attacking other races had long been thrown aside, but their skill in laying traps along a road or pathway was still going strong.

It was nothing but bad news for Glenn.

"Now then, Doctor. How about I do something good for you?"

Arahnia extended her hands. Before he knew it, threads of her silk spun around his body and lifted him upwards with ease. Then he was inverted in midair so that he was facing Arahnia upside down.

With manipulation of the nearly invisible threads of silk, Arahnia could control the space around them at her will. She had the dexterity of an acrobat in a circus troupe.

"Something good... What's that mean?" Glenn asked.

"Oh, come now, Doctor. You know that can only mean one thing between a man and a woman. I couldn't say such an embarrassing thing like that myself, you know."

"Why, though? You and I don't even know each other that well."

"Oh, that *is* true, isn't it? Personally, I am not very interested in the doctor's personality," Arahnia said with a nonchalant look on her face.

The two extra arms extending out from underneath the other two still had shears in their hands. She played with her shears—*snip, snip*—as she answered.

"I'm a dress designer. No one puts more pride and fervor into clothing than me. But, perhaps because of this personality of mine, I don't really have a lot of friends, you know."

"F-friends?"

"You see, it's in my nature to want what others have."

Snip, snip.

The sound of the scissors didn't stop. Glenn wondered if he was going to be spider food, or if he would instead be cut into a piece of fabric. Either way, it seemed clear to him that he wouldn't be able to escape scot-free.

"Ever since I can remember, I've ended up wanting the things held precious by the people I grow close to. Stuffed animals, ornaments—and clothing, too."

"By 'wanting,' you mean...you take it?"

"Oh no, of course not. I don't really want to *take* it. It's just, you know, I want to share the same things they have... I want to match."

"...Even though you're a designer?"

Glenn pondered to himself. She was someone with the vision to make clothes unlike anything anyone else wore and yet, Arahnia seemed elated by her own words as she continued to speak.

"It's probably *because* I'm a designer. The things that are made with these fingers of mine, these nails, these threads—they're each one of a kind. But by creating them, you see, this heart of mine gets lonely easily."

"Okay..."

"I'm sure if I were able to match up with the people I'm close to, I'd be able to create even better designs... Yes, for example..."

Her long-nailed fingers brushed up against Glenn's cheek.

Arahnia's upside-down face drew right up to Glenn's nose.

"Matching lovers, perhaps..."

This, Glenn thought, was very bad.

Arahnia had a serious illness. However, her illness was beyond Glenn's field of expertise—the incurable disease of being

an artist. Its sufferers were far too gone to cure, so obsessed with their particular field that they were prepared to do anything for the sake of creaking a fine piece of art.

Many people were affected by this disease, monster and human alike. Most went to the grave without ever being cured.

I see, Glenn thought to himself, *she is indeed a hardworking person.*

Her focus on doing anything for the dresses she designed was so overly enthusiastic it crossed into the realm of abnormality and absurdity.

"Sapphee and I are nothing more than doctor and assistant. We don't have that sort of a rela—"

"Indeed. Sapphee, you see, has a surprisingly sweet side to her. You're so precious to her, she can't really make her move, it seems."

In actuality, there had been a number of times when things between them had gotten dangerous, but Glenn thought that was beside the point right now.

"I'll make it clear, Doctor: I don't have even an ounce of feelings for you."

"S-so it seems."

"But Sapphee is my dearest friend, and I want things to stay that way. That's why I'm so very interested in the doctor that she's so enamored with." Arahnia licked her lips, and a dubious gleam sparkled in her eyes.

In the east, arachne were called jorougumo. It was said that, in the past, they changed into the shape of a woman and tricked men. However, the origin of that myth was a trivial mystery. The word jorougumo had always referred to the half-spider, half-woman arachne.

Glenn, however, thought that the fiendish seduction of men by arachne seemed to be alive and well.

"If I were to rape you here, Doctor...what do you think would happen?"

"Sapphee would be angry, clearly."

"That's right. And more than that, she would feel endangered and become impatient, right? She'd think, *Oh, no—Dr. Glenn was taken by Arahnia, I can't stay idle anymore... I have to do something before it's too late.* Tee hee hee." Arahnia's shoulders trembled as if she was convulsing. It seemed to Glenn she couldn't stop herself from laughing.

"Oh my goodness, what a story! Her precious doctor, taken from her by her best friend! Sapphee surely wouldn't let herself be defeated, but would instead share her bed with you, wouldn't she?! With this, we'd be sucked into a futile love triangle. With our obsessive love, Sapphee and I would be connected to each other through you, Doctor! Sapphee wouldn't be able to escape from me, not ever!"

"Miss Arahnia, no matter how you justify it, that's a warped way of thinking about it."

"That's true. But you know, Doctor? Perversion is important to creation. The distorted inspiration is what will further radical-ize and intensify my designs! It will serve as the aid I need to cre-ate clothing marvels the likes of which this world has yet to see."

It was absolutely insane logic.

However, the troubling part of Arahnia's personality was that her awareness and continuance of her dark side meant she had deemed that darkness acceptable. Awkward attempts at persuasion wouldn't get through to her.

Glenn wanted to do something to escape, but the threads restraining him were strong. At this rate, he realized, he might actually cross *that* line with Arahnia.

"Now then, Doctor. Give yourself to me. Don't you worry at all—I'm quite confident in my body."

Her body *was* outstanding. The liberally open-breasted clothes she was wearing gave a good glimpse at her degree of self-esteem. Her black hair gently brushed against Glenn's cheek.

The more Glenn twisted his body in an attempt to untie the threads of silk, the more the threads firmly bit into him. Glenn realized there wasn't anything more he could do. He even began to consider how he would apologize to Sapphee as he desperately averted his face from Arahnia's to avoid her incoming kiss, when—

"This! Is! Divine! Punishmeeeeeeent!"

A flash of light streaked through the air, the unmistakable slashes of steel drawn through the sky. The many layers of cutting lines would cut Glenn's body to pieces—or so he thought.

"Awaaah!" he cried.

"There we go," the voice said.

His body no longer supported, Glenn fell. Before he crashed into the earth, however, his body was caught in a sturdy grip.

"Doctor? Are you injured?"

"M-Miss T-Tisalia?!"

The centaur princess had caught him with ease, almost like she was boasting about her strength. There was a longsword affixed to her waist, which she had most likely used to cut Arahnia's threads of silk and release Glenn from his restraints.

"Hmph. This troublesome web isn't anything to worry about when I have a sword in hand. It's a good thing I borrowed it from Kay before I came."

"What are you doing here...?" Glenn asked.

"I hunted you down," Tisalia said, with an innocent look on her face. "I heard everything. Honestly, what a terrible thing you've been through."

"I'm sorry, Tisalia. I always seem to be causing trouble for you... But can you put me down now?"

"Oh? I wanted to keep you in my arms a bit longer."

Glenn couldn't help but feel ashamed at being forever held in the arms of a woman like Tisalia. Not only that, but the two large bulges on Tisalia's chest were strongly asserting themselves against Glenn's body.

With a dissatisfied look, Tisalia quickly placed Glenn on the ground.

"Well, well—it's the young Scythia daughter, is it not?" Arahnia said. "I was sure I'd set up traps to ensure we wouldn't be followed..."

"Hmph. I cut down all those traps of yours." Tisalia pointed her sword toward Arahnia without any hesitation. Looking closely at her, it became evident that both the sword and Tisalia herself were covered in Arahnia's threads of silk.

Even when dirtied with webs, the dignified expression on the centaur's face didn't change.

"I heard everything! Your actions were dubious, but I wouldn't have had anything to say if they came from feelings of love and longing for Dr. Glenn... But instead, what?! You aren't interested in him at all?! You were going to rape the doctor just for your *clothing designs*?! I will *never* allow you to do something so outrageous!"

"I don't really need your permission, though, do I?" Arahnia crossed her four arms as she dangled from a tree.

"I won't overlook such depraved immorality!"

"I'm not very good at handling these types of women, you know..." Despite her words, Arahnia observed Tisalia with a grin on her face.

Tisalia's sword could cut through Arahnia's silk. Arachne had a sturdy exoskeleton and were quite nimble but didn't have much muscular strength. It was clear that if they were to fight head to head, Arahnia was at a disadvantage.

The rank-three arena fighter Tisalia Scythia was already prepared for combat. The lack of an opening in her stance showed she was just as comfortable wielding a sword as she was with her spear.

"I would appreciate it if you didn't interfere," Arahnia said. "This doesn't have anything to do with you, does it, Miss?"

"It absolutely does! After all, I intend on having the doctor here come for a marriage interview and become the heir to the Scythia business!"

"Well, now. So, you're *also* planning on taking him for yourself then, aren't you? You want the doctor to inherit your company. I want the doctor for my own hobby and work. You're no different, are you?"

"Hng...?! N-no, you're wrong! It's true I want a successor for my family's business, but I actually love Dr. Glenn! It isn't strange to get married to the person you love."

"Hmm, but do you really love him? Haven't you just put yourself under the illusion of loving the doctor because he's someone who happened to be nearby and who would be a good fit as a successor?"

"I-I know for certain that's not true!" There was an uncertainty in Tisalia's eyes, and the point of her sword wavered.

Figuring that she couldn't win in a fight, it seemed that Arahnia had changed her strategy, shifting their battle into a war of words.

Arahnia turned her fingertip towards Tisalia and began spinning it in circles. It almost looked like a technique used to confuse and capture dragonflies, but it seemed having an effect on Tisalia.

"You're saying you love Dr. Glenn even without your family's affairs being involved? In that case, why don't you just throw it all away and elope with him?"

"P-preposterous. I have a responsibility to the Scythia family legacy... I could never do that to Kay and Lorna, either..."

"Well then, you're not different from me at all. Our means and ends are both the same, are they not? We both want the doctor for ourselves."

"Th-that's not true. You're, after all, you're...!" Tisalia's sword was trembling violently. The distress their conversation was causing was clear as day.

"Miss Tisalia." Glenn spoke up, realizing the danger. However, he was lost as to what he should say to her. Until now, Glenn had always come up with some sort of excuse to decline Tisalia's invites for a marriage interview. He thought that if a man like him were to try and cheer on Tisalia's love, it would come across as nothing but superficial.

Despite Glenn's wavering, Tisalia's sword moved.

"Just... just..."

"Just?"

"Just! Beeeeee! Quieeeeet!"

"Miss Tisalia?!" Glenn shouted.

The centaur princess moved.

She swung mercilessly at Arahnia with a diagonal slash. Arahnia seemed to have predicted the attack and used her threads to quickly run away.

Tisalia's skill with a sword was wonderful, but Arahnia's speed as she fled was extraordinary. Despite Glenn's earlier assumption, Arahnia seemed surprisingly familiar with scenes of battle and bloodshed.

"That was...a close one!" Arahnia said. "What in heaven's name are you doing?!"

"Shut up, shut up, shut up! Quiet! Stop chattering along with that complicated logic of yours! I don't understand anything about love myself! I've never even really been properly in love before, okay?!"

"Don't sound so proud about it!"

"Never. The. Less!" Tisalia thrust her sword towards Arahnia, who was hopping to-and-fro as she escaped deeper into the woods. "Even though that's the case! I knew at first sight that Dr. Glenn was the one! I won't let you say my feelings are all an illusion! I'm different from someone like you, who said she didn't have *any* feelings of love for him! We're not the same at *all*!"

"Ahhh... I really am no good with these types..." Arahnia groaned, as if this time she was truly having a hard time dealing with Tisalia.

However, she readied her scissors and confronted Tisalia directly. Glenn had thought for sure she would run away, but it seemed she had some intention of fighting. He wondered if she was going to fight with her scissors and if the arachne species, so accustomed to sewing, could also apply their technique to battle.

"Hold on a second, you two—take it easy with the violence," he said.

"Doctor! It became violent a long time ago! From the moment you were captured!" Tisalia said.

It didn't seem that they were going to let Glenn act as a peacekeeper. Tisalia's excuse was understandable, and the excessive lengths Arahnia had gone to were more than enough to force an altercation.

Glenn wondered what he should do. He wanted the two of them to avoid getting injured as much as they possibly could— that was his instinct as a doctor, after all. He had been subjected to a terrible experience at Arahnia's hands, but that didn't mean he wanted her to be hurt. But with both Tisalia's sword and Arahnia's scissors involved, Glenn was sure that neither of them would walk away unharmed if they clashed.

"Fine. I suppose the ends justify the means, then," Arahnia said.

"I *hate* people like you who don't consider those around them!"

Ultimately, Glenn knew that he needed to stop them, even if it meant risking his own life. As Glenn stood there, observing them closely, and bracing himself to interfere—

"Both of you." The voice was icy cold.

Everyone froze as if they had been doused by a bucket of ice water—especially Arahnia, whose face drained of blood.

"You've said some *very* selfish things arguing over *my* Dr. Glenn."

Slither, slither, slither.

From the trees above, a white rope-like something coiled around Glenn. It felt more comfortable than the silk threads. Having already experienced that very touch many times before, Glenn knew it was Sapphee's serpentine lower body.

But today, her coiling was not gentle. From what he could tell, the tail that entangled itself around him, even up to his neck, was using all of its strength.

"Quiet. Quiet. Miss Tisalia, Arahnia, both of you! Just be quiet with all your talk of love or whatever!" A lamenting tone rose in Sapphee's words.

Glenn thought it was probably a cry of exhaustion and frustration, driven forth by all the hard work she'd been doing since

arriving in the village. As she squeezed him with all of her might, he found he couldn't stand to look her in the eye.

"It seems like you don't understand, so I'll be sure to make it perfectly clear—Dr. Glenn does not have *any time at all* to be taken up with love, relationships, or marriage meetings!"

Lamias didn't have tear glands. Even in sorrow, they didn't have the physical makeup to cry any tears. However, if Sapphee had been able to cry, her face right then would likely have been drenched in tears. Those were Glenn's thoughts as his mind grew hazy from lack of oxygen.

Sapphee was unable to cry, but that didn't mean that she wasn't suffering or in pain...

Glenn sincerely berated himself for being such a hopeless man and not realizing that sooner.

✖ ✖ ✖ ✖ ✖

With the arrival of Saphentite Neikes on the scene, the one-on-one combat about to break out between Tisalia and Arahnia had stopped before it could even begin. Glenn fainted from a lack of oxygen, but only for a second. Sapphee quickly came to her senses and released her hold on Glenn. Thus, the situation came to an anti-climactic close. The only remnant of the altercation was the imprint of Sapphee's scales on Glenn's neck.

Arahnia made her escape, and Tisalia politely apologized to Sapphee.

From Sapphee's point of view, it would have made more sense

for Arahnia to apologize to her. She'd had no reason to expect an apology from Tisalia. After all, the centaur had drawn her sword in defense of Glenn.

There, Tisalia came to understand. She understood now the significance of Sapphee's attitude, and why the lamia had been able to rush to Glenn's aid when he was in a pinch.

From the very first moment Sapphee had met with Arahnia in the forest, she had known that Arahnia would have her sights set on Glenn.

✗　✗　✖　✗　✗

"I'm so very sorry, Doctor," Sapphee said. "Truly."

"It's fine. I know you didn't do it on purpose.

"Even still...those marks..." Sapphee had a look of worry on her face as she stared at the marks around Glenn's neck.

The shape of her scales was freshly imprinted on his skin, but it was nothing more than a bruise that would disappear in a few days. Glenn regretted driving Sapphee over the edge so much that he didn't give a single thought about the bruises.

Besides, if Sapphee had actually strangled him with everything she had, the bones in his neck would have been broken. Glenn was confident that there was a certain level of force that she would not go beyond.

"More importantly," Glenn said, "being apologized to while you're busy drinking seems a little disingenuous..."

"I wouldn't be able to bear this situation without drinking!"

Sapphee said and took a swig of the wine in her glass.

She had finally opened the wine Tisalia had given her in exchange for examining and treating Lorna. It was a limited edition white wine from the Alraune Plantation—an extremely expensive bottle not easily acquired unless one was from a rich family like Tisalia. Sapphee hadn't even waited until they were back in Lindworm before opening it up.

Glenn supposed he couldn't be too surprised, though. She was called a drinker because she immediately drank any alcohol she had in her possession, after all.

"More importantly—about Miss Arahnia. Did you know that she was plotting something?" he asked.

"Well, she is my close friend." A self-deprecating smile came to Sapphee's face. "I wouldn't say she was scheming. She's always had a covetous personality. She had heard about you before, so...I figured this would happen sooner or later."

"Really?"

"Yes. It was something I had been expecting. That and the fact that Arahnia and Miss Tisalia definitely wouldn't get along."

Her face growing redder by the minute, Sapphee poured wine into Glenn's glass.

Glenn peeked out of the window of the clinic. The first snow of the season was coming down lightly. It had arrived much earlier than usual. Glenn was sure it wouldn't pile up immediately and close off the mountain road, but the falling snow still served as an announcement that it was time for them to depart—to go home to their clinic in Lindworm.

"I'm...scared," Sapphee said, also looking out at the snow. "Actually, I wasn't even worried about Arahnia. Even if she did take you away from me."

Urkh! "W-wait a second, Sapphee." He'd just been enjoying the taste of the high-quality wine. When he heard her words, he came dangerously close to spitting it all up.

"I mean, she's not serious. Even if your bodies became one, your hearts absolutely wouldn't join with them."

"W-well, I suppose that's true."

That arachne was just infatuated with her interest in Sapphee and her own art. If Glenn had to put it into words, he was nothing more than a tool to her—something to give her inspiration. In a way, it was extremely easy to figure her motives out. It made complete sense that Sapphee had been able to predict Arahnia's plan.

A hedonistic Arachne. She was most likely still in the village, and Glenn wondered what she was doing at that moment. He didn't think he'd be very surprised if she greeted Sapphee and Glenn with an innocent look on her face the next day.

Sapphee said Arahnia was a close friend, but Glenn wondered if she said that precisely because she had come to grips with that self-serving part of Arahnia's personality.

"I love you, Doctor."

Glenn couldn't help but be embarrassed at hearing these words said straight to his face. He should have already been aware of Sapphee's feelings for him, but the redness in his face was certainly not just a result of the wine he was drinking.

Immediately after she looked Glenn in the eye, Sapphee covered her face and beat the air energetically with her tail.

"Despite that...! Despite that, more rivals keep showing up!"

"Th-there really aren't that many..."

"There are! There absolutely are! Dr. Cthulhy and Miss Tisalia! Those two are already more than troublesome enough!"

"I don't really think Dr. Cthulhy has any interest in me anymore..."

"That is *definitely* not true!" Sapphee shook her head vehemently. She was completely drunk.

Glenn thought to himself that he had been right to give Sapphee some time off. She was normally a woman who hid her true feelings. It was good for her to make this time to have a drink and allow herself to let loose. It really was true that her exhaustion had built up inside of her ever since coming to the village.

Therefore, she had a couple of drinks and whined like a petulant child.

"It seems that someday someone might really take you from me, Doctor."

"...Sapphee."

"Arahnia won't capture you. But Miss Tisalia is serious. She's just a little clumsy when it comes to love and romance, and always acts earnestly because of that."

Glenn agreed with that statement. Tisalia was straightforward and never said anything vague or superficial. The number of times she had invited him to a marriage interview was evidence enough of just how serious she was.

However, Glenn had the clinic. If Glenn married her, entered into Tisalia's family, and became the company's heir, he would have to cast aside all the responsibilities he had undertaken. It wasn't something he could agree to at a moment's notice.

"Arahnia truly always manages to stir up trouble." Resting her head in her hand, Sapphee let out a sigh. Her tail swayed quickly back and forth, an indication of her emotional disarray.

It was odd that even with her drinking, she didn't coil herself around Glenn like usual. She was probably worried because she had strangled Glenn earlier that day. Sapphee regretted the fresh scale marks on Glenn's neck more than even he did.

There wasn't anything else Glenn could do, so he gulped down his wine in one swig. He wasn't very good with alcohol. Even just a half a bottle of wine could get his head spinning, but without liquid courage, he wasn't sure he'd be able to tell Sapphee what was on his mind.

"Hey, Sapphee?"

"Yes?"

"I still have the clinic, and I don't know how a lot of things are going to play out in the future, but...there is one thing that I can promise you. You're the only one who I ever share a drink with, Sapphee." Despite being timid, with the liquor in his stomach, Glenn finally managed to get those words out to Sapphee, almost blushing with embarrassment.

The words were equally embarrassing for Sapphee. Her whole face—even her ears—grew bright red. She couldn't look at Glenn, averting her eyes left and right. Her tail frantically swung back and forth.

"Th-th-th-those... those kind of words aren't going to deceive me!"

"You're too loud. Sapphee. You're going to wake up the fairies."

In actuality, Glenn already sensed a gaze staring out from the corner of the clinic. It made sense that the fairies would be curious about all the noise, believing that their work for the day should have already been over.

"W-well, that's because you said something so embarrassing! H-honestly!"

"Yes, yes, it's my fault. I'm a little tipsy, too—why don't we head to bed?"

"O-okay. Oh no, the wine's already all gone..."

Sapphee had been the one to drink most of it, but despite that, she was still reluctant to part from the bottle. She had drunk a considerable amount, but Glenn supposed that for her to still be unsatisfied was only to be expected of a heavy drinker like her.

At that moment, Glenn realized something—something moving. He'd glimpsed it out of the corner of his eye as it moved across the room.

"......?"

As he had assumed, the small shadow belonged to the clinic's helper fairies. But with their work for the day over, it was out of the question that they would be working extra. They were extremely strict with both their work and their payment. They would *never* work beyond what they had been paid to do.

It didn't seem that they were reacting to the uproar that Sapphee was making, but then he saw another fairy crossing the edge of the room. They all seemed to be moving toward the clinic's entrance. Glenn wondered why. They had nothing to do; there was no reason for them to go outside—

Wait, Glenn thought, *that's not it.*

Perhaps this was like when rats fled from a sinking ship—

"...?!"

"Aaaaaaaaaaaaaaaaah?!"

The clinic rocked violently.

The wine bottle on top of the table fell to the floor and shattered loudly.

"E-earthquake?!" Sapphee shouted.

"Sapphee, we need to get outside!"

The trembling was gone in an instant.

A number of things on the clinic shelves had fallen down, but they couldn't worry about them now. They had to get somewhere safe while they still could—but just before the thought came to Glenn's mind, there was another violent quake.

"Eeek!!" Sapphee shrieked.

The trembling was a shock even to Glenn, who wasn't as bad with earthquakes as Sapphee. Somehow, he kept his composure and tried to guide her out. The rumbling came again intermittently after that.

Intermittently? Glenn wondered to himself.

"Sapphee, hurry!"

"O-okay!"

Thinking the whole situation strange, Glenn quickly left the clinic with Sapphee and headed outside.

* * **✖** * *

Glenn and Sapphee managed to find temporary relief in the village square, where there wasn't anything around that could fall on top of them. The residents of the village had all gathered there, and everyone had a distressed look on their face. Tisalia and Arahnia were there, as well.

The rumblings hadn't let up. However, having come from a region that often experienced earthquakes, Glenn came to a realization: These weren't earthquakes at all.

The ground was, without a doubt, trembling. However, the intermittent vibrations were beating out in a fixed rhythm. It was almost as if a giant or something similar were walking along, pounding the ground with its feet, one step at a time.

That can't be, Glenn thought.

"Dr. Glenn, are you all right?" the village elder asked, catching sight of him.

"Oh, yes—yes, I am. It seems to be a big earthquake—has anyone been hurt?" Glenn asked as a reflex. It was half-instinctual, simply part of his nature to worry more about the injuries of other people than his own safety—even in times like this.

"Fortunately, no one's been harmed by these quakes. However..." The village elder hesitated.

Again, the square shook violently. The tremor was over in

an instant. Glenn knew he was right now—this wasn't a regular earthquake.

"I dispatched one of the young harpies to the mountain summit," the elder continued. "I think that this quake—I don't think *any* of the recent tremors have been earthquakes."

"They aren't earthquakes," Glenn mused. "In that case, what could they possibly be?"

"It's an old story," the village elder told Glenn, a hard look on his face. "I'm sure this is the rage of the legendary Giant God, who is said to have dwelt in the Vivre Mountains since ages past."

It sounded almost like a fairy tale, but the village elder's eyes were completely serious.

"According to the report from the young harpy who just returned, there is someone with a body far larger than that of any man approaching the village from the summit, the rumblings of the earth accompanying them as they move."

Glenn's face went pale.

He couldn't believe such an outrageous story, but as soon as that thought came to him, another large tremor rocked the earth, as if it were laughing scornfully at Glenn's disbelief. Sapphee's shoulders trembled in fright, and Glenn gently nestled up close to her.

The rumbling of the earth sounded from far away.

Glenn heard them as the roars of the giant that the young harpy had laid eyes on.

CASE 04:
Attack on Gigas

WITH A GRIM LOOK on his face, the village elder told them of an old legend that had been passed down in the village.

In the age of the ancient gods, long before monster or human existed in the world, there had been a race of giants, ten times larger than a human, known as the gigas. They were colossal, cruel, and brutal. They ate anything and everything—not out of hunger, but out of avarice. If they were given an offering, it brought the benefit of a good, abundant harvest. However, those who didn't give them offerings were tormented with relentless and unsparing violence.

At long last, when the tyranny of the gigas could no longer be overlooked, the gods admonished the gigas. Not only did they ignore their warnings, they revolted against the gods in an attempt to take their place.

The battle between the giants and the gods ended with the gods victorious.

The wild, violent race of giants was locked up in the center of the continent. In order to prevent them from escaping, the gods placed mountains on top of them as stone weights to keep them down.

The mountains that were piled on top of the giants became the steep peaks of the Vivre Mountains.

Even now, the giants suffered under the weight of the mountains. Still, they held onto their power even as they remained sealed within. They became gods that protected those who properly served them—and evil gods who brought disaster to the village when those duties were neglected.

It was the kind of regional guardian deity myth one could find anywhere. However, upon hearing that three hundred years ago, even before the war broke out between monsters and humans, the village had once been completely destroyed, the village elder hadn't been able to laugh off this legend as fantasy.

The Giant Gods, the gigas, truly did exist. And not only that, this being was clearly a walking disaster, capable of destroying the village.

The destruction had happened three hundred years ago, so the village elder didn't know if it was an accurate story or not. However, the Giant God of the gigas that appeared in the village and destroyed houses with their colossal body had nevertheless reduced the harpies to terror.

In the time since then, the village had erected a small shrine and now made offerings to the Giant God without fail. For they knew that if they forgot to give their offerings, the Giant God would again grow hungry and attack the village.

"I thought that it might have been just a fairy tale." With snow falling around them, the village elder spoke as though he were warning children against doing something bad. "And even if it weren't a fairy tale…I thought that if we did our best to make offerings to the Giant God, there wouldn't be any disasters. Why is the Giant God angry now…? Did we do something that offended him?" The village elder frowned. His dread of the giant advancing step by step towards the village was clear.

Glenn pondered. Among the many species of monsters, there *were* some known as giants. Cyclopes and ogres were some of the races referred to as giants—but even though they were large, they were still only about two to three times the size of a human. He had never heard of a monster whose height was over ten times that of a human.

Once again, the earth shook. The houses built into the bluffs that flanked either side of the village collapsed with a loud crash. Cries rose up from the harpies gathered in the village square. Although they were out of danger themselves, Glenn was sure it wasn't a pleasant feeling to watch their homes collapse.

Just like the village elder, other harpies were in a state of panic.

"The Giant God is coming to the village?"

"No way, that can't be true."

"But one of the young ones said they actually saw it."

"Impossible, why would the Giant God attack the village?"

"How the hell would I know? More importantly, what are we going to do?"

Glenn could hear the stream of back-and-forth questions from the villagers. The legend of the Giant God was familiar to everyone in the village.

A question came to Glenn's mind: What would happen if the Giant God, ten times larger than a human, really were to come to the small village? After all, the giant's footsteps were capable of tearing down houses. If the giant actually arrived in the village, the harpies would not be able to escape the destruction.

They had to run—they had no other option.

"Listen up!" In the middle of the square, someone raised their voice above the disorder. Their tone was loud and clear. It was Tisalia, crossing her arms and puffing out her chest. "This is a village emergency! Everyone calm down and act with composure! First...Illy!"

The young girl with vivid wings shuddered in surprise at hearing her name called out so suddenly.

"A-ah?! What?!"

"First, I want to tell the Lindworm City Council what's happening. Miss Skadi should be in the assembly hall even this late at night. She knows your face, so you're best for the job. Get yourself together quickly! Fly to Lindworm!"

"O-okay! Leave it to me!"

Illy flew off immediately, as instructed.

They were fitting instructions, Glenn thought. Both Skadi and her bodyguard Kunai were very familiar with Illy. If she flew into the assembly hall with an emergency announcement, there was no fear she would be turned away.

"Those able to fly, please get your things together quickly! Evacuate to Lindworm!"

At these words, a light kindled in the eyes of the confused and agitated harpies. So long as there were reliable instructions flying about during the chaos, bodies would start moving. Tisalia's loud, clear voice made the harpies understand exactly what they needed to do.

"Kay, Lorna!"

"Yes, Mistress," Kay said.

"We are always at your side," Lorna added.

"Help everyone who can't fly to evacuate. After that, prepare and pack the carriage, okay? As fast as you can. Next is...you, spider woman!"

"Well now, that's quite an eccentric way to refer to someone, isn't it?" Watching closely over the situation with her four arms crossed was Arahnia. As she spoke, she unfolded an arm and scratched her head.

"I figured you'd just run away on your own."

"Well, I am an outsider here. I'd be fine going off somewhere to stay out of the way, but...Sapphee's here, too, after all. I'd like to do anything I can to help."

"In that case, pack the villagers' belongings together! Pack them as tightly as possible!"

"Yes, of course." Arahnia nodded her head with unexpected obedience. Even now, Glenn couldn't get a good grasp on her personality.

"I have something I need to discuss with you, village elder,"

Tisalia said. "I'd like to make arrangements with you now to ensure the evacuation proceeds quickly."

"H-hmm. Understood."

She now had the presence of an army general. Glenn stared at Tisalia, dumbfounded. He had thought she had a weak side to her, but even faced with a dilemma, she was dignified. Glenn was greatly impressed with Tisalia for taking hold of the situation without causing any more chaos.

"And Doctor!"

"Y-yes!"

"Help with the harpies who can't fly. If necessary, treat them so they'll be able to get down the mountain. If they aren't able to walk on their own, I can carry them in the carriage, but...there's a limit to how many can fit. I'd like for as many of them as possible to walk. We don't have much time; please be quick!"

"Understood. I'll do everything I can."

"Is that fine with you as well, Miss Sapphee?"

Sapphee gave a reassuring nod.

Glenn thought their inability to leave the mountain more quickly might have actually been a stroke of good luck. Thanks to their delay, he had yet another opportunity to use his skills with medicine to help others.

Even in an unprecedented situation, such as this invasion by the Giant God, Glenn found that the skills and knowledge he had fostered in his clinic somehow helped him keep calm. Glenn was a doctor, however, so he *had* to keep his composure. Like Tisalia, in dire situations, he had to focus on the things that needed to be taken care of.

"Now, then, everyone—just as I said. Let's move!" Tisalia's voice sounded almost as if she were signaling the start of a battle.

Their objective wasn't victory, however, but escape. In order to begin that escape, Glenn and everyone else in the village began moving at once.

✕　✕　✕　✕　✕

Harpies had a primarily migratory nature. Originally, they had been a species that crisscrossed the continent in search of a comfortable place to rest. The harpy village itself had at first been the colony of a migratory group of harpies who decided the location would be a good place to live peacefully and rest their wings.

Perhaps because of that, the harpies didn't feel extremely attached to the village. Unconcerned with the decision to flee the village, there wasn't any sense of despair on their faces.

"It's because Lindworm is our home away from home," one of the younger harpies said. "For now, we'll escape to Lindworm—we can just come back later if the Giant God calms down."

The harpy who had spoken was one of the ones who had injured her wings several days ago during the unrelenting earthquakes. She couldn't fly, but she was young, and her legs were strong. Glenn didn't think she would have any difficulty walking on the mountain road. He listened to her talk as he examined her wings.

From the beginning, the wooden houses had been built with the assumption that they would quickly fall apart. Taking nothing but money and whatever clothes they could carry, the harpies quickly flew from the village.

The village elder had said the village had been ruined at the Giant God's hands once before. Glenn thought the harpies' ability to quickly accept the inevitable might actually be one of the biggest reasons the village went on to survive.

Illy had been the first to leave and those who had been swift to finish their preparations had departed for Lindworm, as well. So long as they could fly through the sky, even the steep mountain road wasn't a problem for the harpies. Carrying nothing more than the minimum amount of belongings, the evacuating harpies were quite nimble.

There was one person who was integral to the speed of the evacuation.

"Okay, next! Now, now, keep them coming for me!"

It was Arahnia Taranterra Arachnida.

Instructed to bundle all of the villagers' belongings together, she was now steadily wrapping their things together with her threads. Tying clothing and loose change together, her skilled legs and arms piled many layers of silk one on top of one another, until they'd been fashioned into a square.

These square masses of silk were light and easy to carry—and easy to store, on top of that. Packing each person's belongings together like this one at time, Arahnia was steadily moving the evacuation forward.

"Thanks to my silk, your belongings will be safe, even if you drop them. No need to worry about them while you're flying, now."

Glenn had thought that she had an entirely self-serving personality, but he couldn't see anything egotistic about her as she helped the harpies. She appeared to be a surprisingly good-natured woman, so long as her work wasn't involved. Still, her habit of throwing away all ethics and morals when it came to her work *was* a problem.

Glenn's job was proceeding decently, as well. The night had already grown late, but with the help of Sapphee and the helper fairies, he was examining everyone in the village. That said, Glenn didn't have much work to do for the evacuation. Most of it consisted of strapping babies to their mothers' backs with thread and handing out sturdy canes to the elderly harpies.

Sapphee was also handing out emergency-use medicine to their patients. If anything, Glenn thought that she was even busier than he was. When disaster struck, food and water were of the utmost importance, but the sick running out of their daily medicines was another problem that had to be faced. On top of that, while she worked hectically, Sapphee also hastened to pack together their things for the return to Lindworm.

Glenn had finished up his patient examinations for the most part when Kay came bounding over.

"Doctor!" she said.

With her sprain completely healed, she was rushing around the village looking even livelier than she had before the sprain. Glenn was sure that with her and Lorna's help, the evacuation would continue without delay.

"We loaded as many of your medical tools on the carriage as

we could. According to Miss Arahnia, it will be difficult to load any more than what we already have..."

"It's unavoidable. We'll leave the remaining tools here."

"Are you sure?" Kay stared straight at Glenn. Once again, the air about her was subtly different when she was by herself than when she was working together with Lorna. She seemed more virile and androgynous than Lorna. Looking closer, her eyebrows were very imposing on her face, and when she stood with her back perfectly straight, she resembled a knight out of a fairy tale. She gave the impression of a woman who was popular with other women.

It was a mysterious air to have, though, as when she was standing together with Lorna, the two of them seemed like they were twins. The dignified Kay, and the gentle Lorna. The two of them each had their own quirks, yet when they were both together, they truly appeared to be sisters.

"It doesn't matter," he said. "We can always come back and get the tools when everything has calmed down... Even if, worst case, they get lost, we'll order new ones from Kuklo Workshop. Carrying lives is more important than tools."

"Understood. I will do as you say."

Kay courteously bowed her head and took something from a pouch that hung at her waist. She tossed it Glenn's way.

"What is this?"

"Wrapped candy Lorna made here in this village. A steady supply of nutrients is especially important in situations like this. If anything should happen to you, Doctor, everyone in this village will be in grave danger."

"Th-thank you very much."

"Now, then—I am off!"

Once again bowing her head, Kay dashed away. From guiding the refugees to supervising the preparations, she and Lorna had a mountain of things they needed to attend to.

Glenn thought that the consideration she had shown him, despite being busy with all of her work, was indicative of just how capable a handmaiden she was.

"Dr. Glenn," Sapphee said.

"Hm? What is it, Sapphee?"

"The examinations have been finished for the most part." She gave an assured nod. Her saying this meant that now all of the harpies in the village were ready and able to descend the mountain—whether by flying, walking, or being pulled in the carriage by Kay and Lorna.

During all of the preparations, the tremors had never stopped. Yet another house built into the bluff collapsed and fell to the earth. The village elder had said they would later collect the scattered pieces of wood and use them for lumber to remake their houses, but even with those uplifting words in the air, it wasn't going to be an easy feat.

In the meantime, the harpies had all accepted their move to a new address with ease. That was just the type of people they were. They had originally been a species of monster that lived freely, after all, much like the winds that crossed over the continent.

"We should hurry, ourselves," Sapphee said. "We wouldn't stand a chance against this 'Giant God,' if we ran into them."

"That's right..."

A Giant God who could shake the very earth. If their mythic strength was a reality, the Giant was obviously not an opponent humans or normal monsters could deal with. To oppose them head on, they would probably need a dragon at their side. Indeed, if they'd had a dragon with them—such as the fire dragon Skadi Dragenfelt, who lived in Lindworm—they might have been able to tackle even an emergency situation like this with strength of arms.

However, all a mere man of medicine such as Glenn could do was lend a hand to help make the evacuation a quick one.

"That's right," Glenn murmured to himself. "But..." He paused.

"Doctor?"

There was something on his mind that had been bothering him for a while, now. Kay, Lorna, Arahnia, and Sapphee: they were all working in earnest for the sake of the village, yet—

There was one person Glenn couldn't find anywhere.

Glenn had been certain that she was speaking with the village elder, but he was busy issuing instructions to the other harpies. It seemed that their meeting together was over.

"...Doctor. Don't tell me," Sapphee said.

"No, I'm sure it's nothing, but..." Glenn shook his head at the bad hunch he had.

Something had felt off from the start. Tisalia had handed out her instructions to everyone and had put forward a makeshift escape plan but hadn't said anything about what she herself was going to do. Maybe it had been something not worth the trouble of speaking out loud. Maybe it was already clear what she was going to do.

What, then? What was she doing?

They had plenty of people to do what needed to be done. She had been standing there acting as their leader, and now she was gone. What in the world was it that Tisalia Scythia had to do so urgently?

From far off in the distance, Glenn could hear the rumbling of the earth.

Again, the Giant God took another step closer to the village. The tremors seemed to be getting bigger. If that was the case, the evacuation might be hindered.

"In any event, let's keep doing what we can. Right, Sapphee?"

"O-okay," she said, looking alarmed. She seemed perplexed by Glenn's words.

Kay, Lorna, Illy, and Arahnia, who Glenn had thought to be self-righteous and selfish—none of them were from the village, yet they had united as one to find a way out of their predicament. That's how pressing the situation was.

So, what about Tisalia? Glenn wondered. After all, she was the person with the strongest sense of responsibility of them all.

In a crisis such as this, he wondered what in the world it was that she could possibly be doing. Glenn felt that, with some thought, the answer would come to him in due course.

Tisalia Scythia continued along the mountain road, snow falling around her.

She was on the mountain path, but it wasn't a path that led down the mountain. In fact, it was headed in the opposite direction—a path that continued up to the summit. The snow wasn't enough to cover it up but instead soaked and muddied the trail as it fell. However, the centaur's hooves continued forward in defiance of the mud. The horseshoes that Glenn had fitted her with protected her steps no matter what road she walked on.

She had only two of her belongings with her. On her back was her cherished spear. The other thing she carried was a heavy burden of hers—her determination.

Tisalia knew where the Giant God was from the rumblings of the earth. She only had to walk in the direction of the thunderous tremors and the quaking of the ground. She was sure that if it had been the middle of winter, with the snow thick on the mountain, she would have had to be careful to avoid any avalanches. Fortunately, however, the winter was still young. Tisalia continued marching forward, unwavering.

Even if she had staggered along, thanks to the continuous tremors, even if her legs were at times swept out from under her, she had no intention of stopping.

"...I wonder if I should have said something to Dr. Glenn." That was the only regret she had. "But he probably would have stopped me if I had, right?"

Tisalia was going off to meet with the Giant God. *No*, she thought, correcting herself. *This won't be something as simple and easy as merely meeting with the giant.*

Tisalia was headed into battle to stop the Giant God's advance.

The evacuation of the harpies was moving forward quickly with Glenn's help, but it was still too slow. It was especially difficult to imagine that the elder harpies, who were unable to fly, and the children, would be able to evacuate in time. Even if they left the village quickly, if the Giant God had seriously set their sights on the harpies as they descended the mountain—the difference in their gaits was plain to see. Without a doubt, the Giant God would gain on them.

The legend of the Giant God was new to her, but if they were truly ten times the size of a human, their gait would be different, as well. Even if the Giant God was slow and dull, she had no doubt they would catch up with the fleeing harpies.

Someone had to stop the Giant God from advancing, Tisalia—the heiress to the Scythia family and the one who had pledged to lead their clan—was the only one who could do it. So long as she carried her pride as her clan's princess, it was her duty to take up her spear and lead the way in times of crisis. As the princess of the Scythia, who had won their fame as warriors, it had been the natural choice to make. Her decision had been inevitable.

Taking pride in her family's military fame was still beyond her wildest dreams unless she faced battle and her own certain death. Holding both her spear and her own resolve, Tisalia unwaveringly continued up the path leading toward the Giant God.

"...Tee hee." She laughed to herself, sure that, if he'd had the opportunity, Glenn would have asked what she would do if she were killed. Tisalia unconsciously let a laugh escape from her mouth. Asking her what she'd do if she died was a silly question. The second she died, her consciousness would disappear. Anyway, thinking about what would happen at that moment wouldn't help her.

She had to make the most of the present—that was what was most important. At that moment, taking up her spear for the sake of the harpies was Tisalia's purpose—that and her honor.

Naturally, the difference in strength between her and her opponent was undoubtable. Tisalia didn't know what type of being this Giant God was, but if they had caused ruin to the village before, then a mere arena fighter like Tisalia had no hope of holding them at bay.

Still, someone needed to be the village's shield.

Tisalia wondered if anyone else could have done the job besides her. Kay and Lorna, Glenn, even Illy, Sapphee, or even—*actually*, she thought, interrupting herself, *I don't really care what happens to Arahnia*. But the others were all important people to Tisalia. If she wanted to protect them, she herself had be the one to go.

Tisalia gave no thought to what she would do if she died—or anything like that. Instead, she decided to think about what would happen if she were victorious. If she managed to survive, proposing to Glenn sounded like a good idea. No matter how straight-laced he might be, he would surely be moved when presented with the famed and glorious fighter who overcame the

Giant God.

"Hee hee hee hee..." *Indeed,* Tisalia thought to herself, *that didn't sound bad at all.*

Thinking this, she burst spontaneously into high spirits as she approached her near-certain death. It was as if her fantasies had wings and raced through the sky. It was good, she thought, very good.

"Please don't laugh in such a revolting manner."

"Nhgaaah?!"

Out of the blue, something flew towards Tisalia. It was a white snake's tail, bent like a stinging whip, coming right for her face—but the centaur's experience wasn't just for show. She held up her spear at once and brushed aside the white whip. It seemed the attack had been nothing more than a feint, and Tisalia's response to it was a light one.

"Who is it?! No, I know who it is! Miss Sapphee!"

"That's right." The albino lamia appeared without a sound from a copse of trees alongside the road.

Thanks to her lineage as an assassin, Sapphee had been able to sneak up close to Tisalia without revealing her presence. Tisalia, of course, wasn't aware of Sapphee's heritage. Nevertheless, she had a feeling that Sapphee had been trained in some kind of combat skills and techniques.

Tisalia's warrior's intuition had probably been sounding warning bells ever since the two of them met.

"...What in the world is with that big fluffy coat you're wearing?" Tisalia asked.

"It's cold, you know. Arahnia improvised and knitted it for me," Sapphee said nonchalantly, wrapped up in a hooded coat heavy with fur.

Being a lamia, she had a poikilothermic body. No matter how much protection she wore, though, it would probably never be enough—after all, the weather was cold enough for snow.

Ignoring all that, Tisalia had to admit that the arachne woman's workmanship was in fact quite unbelievable. No matter that the coat had been "improvised," she had still created a hooded coat in an extremely limited amount of time.

"Do you intend to go up against the Giant God all by yourself?" Sapphee asked.

"But of course! Times like these call for noblesse oblige, a duty for those who stand above others! Oh ho ho ho!"

"Your ears. They're shaking."

"Ah." Her ears were indeed trembling with anxiety. Having that pointed out to her put Tisalia at a loss for words. No matter how much she puffed out her chest, no matter how resolved she was, her body was still honest. It eloquently revealed her fear of the near-certain death she was approaching. The mere act of steeling herself was itself driven by the fear she held of death. After all—if she hadn't been scared, then there wouldn't have been any need for her to resolve herself to her actions.

"This is very much like you, Miss Tisalia." Another well-known face appeared.

"D-Doctor?!"

"But saying you've prepared yourself to die—well, as a doctor,

I can't overlook that. What would you do if you died?"

Tisalia gave a dry smile as Glenn said exactly what she had imagined he would.

She had known that this would happen—that was why she had slipped out of the village without saying a word to anyone. She didn't actually think that they would chase after her.

"It would be tough by yourself, right? We will back you up," Sapphee said as if it were simply the natural thing to say.

"B-back up?! Are you serious?! You didn't come to try and stop me?"

"You're not the type to listen when others try to stop you— right, young miss horsewoman?" Sapphee took a blade from her breast pocket. It was a deeply curved short sword, used for surprise attacks. There was an elaborate design engraved into the blade, the sort venom could be applied to. Victims of the blade would thus be filled with a large amount of poison.

That was the type of woman Sapphee was. Despite being a town medicine maker, she had taken out her poisoned short sword with unflinching calm. Using poison as a weapon was a double-edged sword, as there was always the chance that the user could die if they made even a single mistake. That Sapphee could calmly wield such a weapon surprised Tisalia.

"You might die," Tisalia said. "I'm more than fine on my own."

"And what if you were trampled without stopping the Giant God at all—what then?" Sapphee asked.

"That's why you two should come with me...? I can't even laugh, the punchline is that we all die in vain."

"Why did you come if you knew you would die in vain, then?" Sapphee was stubborn. Tisalia understood what she was saying.

Saphentite and Tisalia were both very similar. Tisalia thought this was probably why they had grown to love the same person. It was why her relationship with the lamia wasn't just antagonistic. Tisalia also felt a sense of closeness with her.

That was precisely why Tisalia had to make Sapphee back down.

"I need you to protect the doctor and go back down the mountain," Tisalia said. "Who will protect the doctor if you're with me?"

"Now, now, both of you hold on a second." Glenn cut into their endless back and forth to mediate the situation. "I have a bit of an idea."

✖ ✖ ✖ ✖ ✖

The doctor's plan was simple.

Glenn had a thought. Was it really necessary for them to fight the Giant God in the first place? The Giant God in question was just walking at the moment. Its movement had caused earthquakes and made the houses of the village collapse, but that didn't mean the Giant God itself was causing harm to the village. They didn't seem to be doing anything proactively destructive.

It was true that just by walking they were causing damage and that this had made it necessary for the harpies to evacuate. But Glenn wondered if it were really necessary to try and fight the Giant God.

Was it really impossible for them to negotiate with the Giant God?

"A-are you serious, Doctor?" Tisalia asked.

"I'm serious. We'll talk with the Giant God and—if possible—have them stop their movement towards the village."

"We don't even know if they'll understand us!"

"Exactly. We won't know unless we try to talk with them."

Tisalia shook her head, completely flabbergasted.

But Glenn was serious. At the moment, nothing the Giant God was doing seemed malicious. Even if the brutality spoken of in the legends wasn't all a lie, it was likely that they were probably living a quiet life these days. Their personality may have mellowed out a little due to being sealed away by the gods.

Glenn shook his head. Surely that was all nothing more than his own optimism.

"It's just as he said, Tisalia," Sapphee said. Somewhere along the way, she had stopped referring to Tisalia as "Miss" when she spoke. "This is what my Dr. Glenn is like. You told me to run away and protect the doctor, but...that was wrong from the beginning. Dr. Glenn isn't the type of person to run away. He's much more stubborn than the both of us, you know."

"B-but..."

"If he weren't, then I wouldn't have ended up breaking into a slave-trader's hideout."

It hadn't been his intention to get wrapped up in that situation, but—well, none of that mattered now. As long as there were people who might end up getting hurt, there was no way Glenn would run away. None of the three of them had any intention of running, so now that they were gathered together, it would be best to simply head toward the Giant God.

If they managed to convince the Giant God to stop, that would be ideal.

"What will you do, Tisalia?" Sapphee asked.

"...Fine then." Tisalia still had a frown on her face, but she fixed her grip on her spear again. "Understood, Sapphee. Dr. Glenn is the person I fell in love with at first sight. If you insist, then I will agree to your accompaniment... However, when negotiations fail—" Tisalia hoisted her spear and showed a glimpse of her fighting spirit.

On the other side of her, Sapphee wordlessly readied her knife. It was possible that she was better than Tisalia when it came to flexible and adaptable weapons like her deadly poison and short sword—though who knew if her skills in assassination would be effective against a Giant God.

"Of course," Sapphee said. "When the time comes, we'll figure something out. I hope that paralyzing poison will work."

"When you poison them, I'll use that opening to attack," Tisalia said. "Does that sound good, Sapphee?"

"An adequate plan."

Glenn gave a sigh of relief. The two of them were always picking fights with each other whenever they got together, but he knew for certain that their relationship wasn't only filled with hostility. Even when something happened in the village, they both seemed to be worried about one another. Glenn thought it likely they wouldn't join together outside of times like today, but together, the seasoned centaur warrior and the skilled lamia assassin made a good team. Glenn couldn't have asked for a better pair of bodyguards.

He had a feeling that with them both dropping formalities, there was a kind of friendship forming between them, and he heaved a deep sigh of relief. He was positive that it was better for the women he knew well to get along.

Once again, the earth shook. Glenn stiffened and drew close against Sapphee, waiting for the tremors to subside. Now the shaking of the earth had made it hard for them to stand. The fear he had felt from earthquakes was nothing compared to what he faced now.

That said, the intensity of the shaking was proof that the Giant God was close by.

"Here we go, you two."

Keeping her resolve locked in her heart, Tisalia spearheaded their advance.

✖ ✖ ✖ ✖ ✖

The snowstorm grew stronger. The mountain road at last arrived at a ravine between the mountains. The area resembled the village's location, a wide open space flanked on either side by large bluffs.

In the ravine was the Giant God.

"This is, well..." Glenn didn't know what to say.

Amongst the piling snow, the Giant God stood there like a huge tree that had been there since time immemorial. Glenn, Sapphee, and Tisalia all looked up at the size of what was before them and give a long sigh.

It was a giant.

The elder had told Glenn they were ten times the size of a human. But there was a big difference between knowing the numbers and seeing the size in person. The Giant God's overwhelming presence left Glenn and the others at a loss for words.

He couldn't really see the monster's face. The sun had long gone down and long bangs shadowed the Giant God's visage, a fact that only heightened the trio's fear.

The god's body was very similar to a human. However, long white hair grew from both their legs and arms. Glenn wondered if that was because they lived in the snowy mountain. The long hair that stretched out from their head was disheveled, making them look more beast than human.

As for the giant's physique, both of their arms were comparatively big. Their fingers seemed to be thick, as well. The clothes they wore looked sloppily made. *No*, Glenn thought. *Not made. I could search the whole continent and* still *not find any clothes to match the giant's size.*

Instead, the cloth looked patched together, giving an impression of barbarity and wildness.

Some species of monsters in the world resembled monkeys and bears. The giant before them had some physical qualities that resembled those races. Glenn shook his head—no, this appalling size was completely different from any sort of monster he was familiar with. Even ogres and cyclopes, which were often referred to as giants, would never grow to such heights.

However, Glenn thought: *A w-woman?!*

Her ample breasts. The tapering of her waist. Her long hair.

Looking at these parts of her, the Giant God *was* undoubtedly a woman. When he thought about it, it wasn't necessarily strange that she was a woman. It was just that he had been thinking of the Giant God as a man and was surprised at the revelation.

The fact that she is a woman means that they have genders?! In that case, can they have children? If that's so, then...while she's quite different from common races of monster, can her existence be placed within the larger monster taxonomy?!

Glenn's academic interests came to the forefront of his mind, but he shook his head, thinking that now wasn't the time for that. Their first priority was to negotiate with the Giant God standing calmly on the ground in front of them.

"O Giant God! We have something to tell you!" Glenn called out to her. When he received no answer, he said, "Please hear our cries! Your footsteps have terrified the villagers! Why do you now make your way toward the harpy village?!"

Glenn called out again and again but still received no reply. She didn't move at all.

Tisalia readied her spear, and Sapphee held her poisoned knife at her side. The two of them were already prepared for battle.

"What has caused your anger, O Giant God? Please tell us the reason for your wrath!"

Slowly, the Giant God's face turned towards them.

The eyes hidden by her hair met Glenn's for just a moment—or at least, Glenn got the feeling they had. His shoulders shook in surprise at the giant's withering gaze. *So, this is what such a colossal opponent is capable of,* Glenn thought. *Even the strength of her gaze is extraordinary!*

He wondered if it were going to end up being impossible to negotiate. He shut his eyes and gave up. They didn't stand a chance.

Then, at that moment:

"Aaaaaaaaaah." The Giant God said something.

They didn't seem to be words with any meaning to them. Glenn wondered if they would be able to speak with the Giant God, period. Up until that moment, he hadn't considered that possibility.

But if she can *talk, then a conversation might also be feasible,* Glenn thought.

"O, Giant God! Just now, what did you say?!"

"Aaaaaaaaaaah, aaaaaaaaaah!" The giant's body shook intensely. Tisalia and Sapphee began charging at once. Glenn braced himself, thinking the encounter would end in a battle after all, when—

"Aaaaaaaaaaaaaachoooooooooooo!" *Splush*!

Something fell in front of Glenn's eyes. It was about an armful's amount of thick, viscous liquid. It closely resembled a race of monster known as a slime.

But this was different.

It wasn't a slime or anything of that nature. It appeared to be some sort of secretion. It was a splash of either drool or mucus, expelled by the Giant God—something that took Glenn a moment to recognize.

It hadn't harmed him, since it had fallen right before him, but...if he had been hit directly in the head with it... Well, he didn't especially want to think about what that would have been like.

"Um, excuuuuuuuuse me." The voice had a long, drawn out way of speaking, without any feeling of tension or nervousness.

"She talked..." Tisalia muttered, utterly stunned.

Overwhelmed, Sapphee had dropped her poisoned knife. She picked it up with her tail in a fluster.

Glenn wondered what was going on.

"I heeeeeeeeard a doooooooooooctor was in the harpy village, you seeeeeeeeeeee..." the giant said.

"O-okay..." Glenn replied.

They would be able to communicate, then. And not *just* communicate, but communicate with ease. The Giant God's manner of speaking was relatively normal. She spoke slowly and calmly. Her voice echoed from far up in the sky, but that didn't hinder their conversation.

That said, her voice was powerful, and each time she spoke it seemed like her words were slamming into Glenn's body.

"I was thinking I'd like to be exaaaaaaaaaaaaaaaaaaamined. I feeeeeeeeeeeel like I have a cooooooooooooooooold." She gave a loud sniff of her nose.

Glenn had no idea what to say.

The three of them looked at each other, at a loss for words for reasons completely different from what had originally struck them speechless at the Giant God's imposing presence. They wondered what they should do. They had prepared themselves to try and negotiate with the Giant God.

Before they knew it, the snow had stopped.

The Giant God looked troubled and was waving her colossal hands left and right.

The dwarfed human and monsters stood there for a long, long time without giving any answer. The woman known as the Giant God simply sat there in confusion and waited for their reply.

EPILOGUE:
The Town Doctor & the Horsewoman Princess

SKADI DRAGENFELT was a dragon.

There were a multitude of types of dragons, but there were many things they all shared in common. They all had a great power within them, so great that normal living things—such as humans and other species of monster—were no match for them. This power wasn't limited to physical strength; it also included the power of curses and magic.

One thing Kunai Zenow, Skadi's bodyguard, often heard people wonder was whether a dragon like Skadi really needed a bodyguard. However, Kunai's status as a bodyguard was nothing but her public-facing position. There was a group of people who thought that unofficially Kunai and Skadi had some sort of improper relationship, which was why Kunai was always at Skadi's side. Suspicions always haunt the guilty mind, after all. Of course, Kunai always made sure those sorts knew that such wasn't the case—all while she wrung their necks.

There was a reason Kunai had been chosen to be Skadi's bodyguard.

That reason was especially on display at night.

They were in the Lindworm Council Hall, in a private room that had been prepared for Skadi. It contained a bed for light naps, upon which Skadi was now resting. Naturally, her master's face veil was off while she was sleeping. However, her face was covered by the blanket, stubbornly making sure not to show her face to others.

Kunai Zenow sat in a nearby chair with her legs crossed. It was a standard midnight scene for the pair.

"...!"

The glass on the window broke in a loud clamor.

Kunai was quick to move. Her status as the former top-ranked fighter in the arena wasn't just for show. In an explosion of movement, she apprehended the person who had burst through the glass and flown into the room.

"Eeek!" said the intruder.

"Quiet!" Seizing both arms of the intruder, Kunai immobilized her with a joint lock.

Kunai could tell from the feathers fluttering down around her that the intruder was a harpy. The bodyguard thought that her wings were a rather flashy color and mused that it was quite bold of her to try and sneak into Skadi's bedroom with such a conspicuous pair of wings.

It was situations like this that made Kunai's position as Skadi's bodyguard important. Even though Skadi was a dragon, she still needed to sleep. No matter how strong a person was, once they fell asleep they became vulnerable. However, with her body made out of corpses, Kunai Zenow didn't need to eat or sleep. For this reason, she had been assigned to be Skadi's sleepless, ever-wakeful bodyguard.

"Who are you?! You didn't think you'd just be able to sneak into the Lady Draconess's room…did you?"

"Aaaaah! Let me goooo!"

"…It can't be—Illy?"

Kunai let go of Illy in spite of herself, recognizing the face of the intruder as the girl's wings wriggled in her grip.

"That hurt, you know!" Illy shouted. "What do think you're doing?!"

"Suddenly flying in here like that is much worse, isn't it? But… you've gotten very colorful, haven't you?"

"Tee hee hee heee! Beautiful, aren't they?"

With Kunai's hold on her loosened, Illy stood up abruptly and spread out her wings.

Kunai had been the one to make the various preparations necessary to send her to the harpy village, but because of how much her wing color and the shape of her crest had changed, she hadn't realized it was her at first.

She had been told Illy's symptoms were related to molting but couldn't believe the change was so dramatic.

"Wait!" the harpy said. "Now isn't the time for this! This is serious!"

"You're right, this *is* serious. Flying into the Lady Draconess's sleeping quarters like this! It's extremely rude."

"Not that! We have an emergency!"

"Emergency?" Kunai tilted her head in confusion. No matter how pressing the emergency was, Kunai was certain it didn't merit disturbing her master's sleep. However, there was a look of desperation on Illy's face.

"I don't really understand it well, but there's some kind of Giant God? It's coming, they said. Everyone's faces in the village went white when they heard!"

"Oh, right," Kunai said. "You only arrived at the village recently, so I guess you wouldn't know. The old story of the Giant God of the harpy village is a famous one, but—wait a second. Did you just say the Giant God is coming?

"Yup, I did!" Flashing open her wings, Illy repeated her claim.

"But that's just a fairy tale."

"That's what I'm trying to tell you! It's *not* just a fairy tale or a legend! The Giant God is already on its way! Their footsteps are causing earthquakes, the village is close to being attacked, and everyone is escaping to Lindworm! Tisalia told me to get the message to Skadi as quickly as possible!"

"Don't be disrespectful; it's *Lady* Skadi to you," Kunai scolded her, but Illy was looking around restlessly. Kunai figured that she was searching for Skadi.

"Don't worry about that!" Illy said. "We have to prepare somewhere for all the villagers to stay! They'll get here before we're ready if we don't hurry! Actually, the Giant God might come all the way down to Lindworm..."

"If that happens, I'll make sure to turn the tables back on them. For now, I'll speak with the Draconess about it, so just hold on for a moment... Oh." Kunai approached the bed, thinking to herself that she couldn't bear to disturb Skadi as she rested, but her small master was already sitting up on top of the bed. Kunai hurriedly knelt down on one knee.

"Lady Draconess, were you woken up?" Kunai figured she must have been, what with the all the noise Illy had made.

The Draconess Skadi took the veil she always wore from beside her pillow and tied it to the two horns that rose up from the top of her head.

When she was appearing in front of others, she was always wrapped in a long, flowing robe, but now she was only wearing her thin nightwear. The lines of her body made her look like a young girl, but she was far stronger than Kunai. If she were to return to her original body as a fire dragon, Kunai was sure that even she would be like a speck of dirt to her.

"There's no need for worry." Skadi's words came like the sounds of a wind chime.

Her voice was crackled and high pitched, like something metal toppling over. Now that Kunai thought about it, she had never really seen any wind chimes in Lindworm. The characteristics of her voice were peculiar, and it seemed that most people couldn't hear it—just those she was close with. Cthulhy and Kunai, for example, could hear her voice properly.

All in all, Skadi was a delicate character, similar to a piece of crystal glass—in both voice and personality.

"That girl in the Vivre Mountains—she doesn't mean any harm," Skadi said.

"Understood... But what do you mean by 'that girl'?" Kunai asked.

"The Giant God from legends. A gigas. Her fellow gigas gradually declined, but that girl has endured. Normally, she accidentally scares the animals of the forest when she moves around, so she lives quietly in a cave up on the summit... Her going to the village is simply because she has some sort of business there."

"As to be expected of My Lady Draconess, you are quite knowledgeable."

"It was only once, but I've met with her before."

Kunai thought about a dragon visiting with a Giant God. She imagined that they had discussed Skadi's plans to step into the Giant God's territory and govern over the city that was to be built there. Kunai wondered if, much like Skadi's relationship with Cthulhy, who was the descendent of a malevolent god, the long-lived races of monsters all had an understanding amongst one another.

"Her name is Dione Nephilim. Tell her, Kunai. She means no harm."

"Yes, understood."

After bowing her head to her master, Kunai conveyed to Illy everything Skadi had said.

Conveying the words of her master to those who couldn't hear them was yet another duty as her bodyguard. The honor was all Kunai's, and it was impossible for anyone else to do it in her stead.

Without changing a single word or phrase, Kunai passed on what Skadi had said to Illy. But the look of dissatisfaction didn't disappear from Illy's face.

"Mrrr...but it's strange, isn't it?!" Illy asked.

"What is?"

"The village elder—he said that long ago, because of the Giant God, the village was ruined...!"

Kunai *did* remember that sort of story being a part of the harpies' lore. She had thought of the whole story as a fairy tale, though, so she didn't remember the specifics.

"Harpies forget quickly," Skadi said, remaining calm even in the face of Illy's protestations. "The more elaborate details haven't survived over time. The harpies don't worry about the finer parts of a story—that's why these old stories become twisted into their folktales. The part about the gigas revolting against the gods was all added later."

Kunai communicated Skadi's eloquent reply to Illy just as she had heard it.

Illy's eyes grew wide as she listened attentively to Skadi's story. Kunai wondered what it was that always made her audiences listen so raptly. Maybe there was something in Skadi's words that fascinated those who heard them. She supposed it was the charisma necessary to be the representative of a big city like Lindworm.

"The ruin of the village is a lie," Kunai said. "The houses simply collapsed because of Dione's giant steps."

"R-really?"

"That's right. You can return to the village. I'm sure by now—"

There, Skadi's words broke off.

By now? What's going on? Kunai wondered.

Now that she thought about it, that doctor and the Scythia daughter were there in the village. She wondered if they were meeting with the Giant God.

"I'm sure by now, they're having fun." Skadi smiled.

Her face wasn't visible under her veil, but Kunai could still hazard a guess about her change in expression. It was a result of her long years of loyalty, serving as her bodyguard.

Thinking about the fun going on up in the village, Kunai felt a slight longing to join in. Of course, she was a bodyguard, so it was impossible for her to leave Skadi's sight—yet she sensed that even Skadi herself wanted to join in with everyone else and their fun.

In a hurry, Illy took off through the window she had destroyed. Skadi watched her head back to the village as a cold wind blew into the room. Her long tail swung back and forth.

"How about you take yourself to the village, Lady Draconess?" Kunai suggested.

"Unnecessary. My appearance would only bring chaos."

"I'm sure that wouldn't be the case."

"I have you, Kunai—so it's fine."

Kunai bowed her head without saying anything in response to those few short words of trust.

It seemed that there was a slight tinge of disappointment, traces of regret, in her expression, but Skadi simply continued to stare straight out at the mountains that could be seen from the city.

Yet no matter how much of a giant the Giant God was, it was obviously unlikely that they would be able to see her from all the way down in the city.

✖ ✖ ✖ ✖ ✖

The snow had stopped.

In the harpy village that had emptied just the night before, the weather was surprisingly fair. It was as if the snow from the previous day had been a dream.

Everyone in the village had returned to their normal way of life, as if the extreme panic and chaos of the night before had also been nothing but a dream. The young harpies of the village had immediately started to restore the destroyed houses, and those who had flown down to Lindworm were returning one by one.

The reason for all of this was simple. The Giant God, the woman who had introduced herself as Dione Nephilim, had made her lack of hostility clear to all.

"Ooooooooooh! Is this the exaaaaaaaaaaaaaam?"

"Yes, please remain still."

"Okaaaaaaaaaaaaaay."

In the village square, Dione sat with both her knees held in her arms. It seemed she was good at staying still and had been in this pose ever since she arrived in the village.

She had gone the whole night without moving her body. In fact, it might have been harder work for her to come down to the village than it was for her to stay in the same seated position for a long period of time.

"Doctor! Be careful!" Sapphee said.

"I will—I'll be fine!" Glenn smiled as he answered the words of warning from Sapphee, who was down below.

He was standing on top of scaffolding that had been assembled out of wood. The harpies excelled at constructing things with wood and had erected it quickly around Dione where she sat. By climbing up the scaffolding, Glenn was able to get face to face with Dione and speak with her.

Her face alone was bigger than Glenn was tall. It was impossible not to think about how he would be swallowed whole if she were to open her mouth wide. Even so, Glenn knew that—despite her anxiety and apprehension—Dione had a gentle personality. When Illy had returned from Lindworm and given her explanation the night before, it became clear the Giant God meant no harm.

Illy had immediately grown attached to the Giant God and was now sitting on top of her head, playing around. Dione's green, soft, and fluffy hair felt quite nice to the touch. The giant didn't reprimand Illy at all for sitting on top of her head and left her as she was.

"When did you start to feel sick?" Glenn asked.

"Hmmmmmmmmmm? Ummmmmmmmm, ten years agoooooo?"

"...That's right around when Lindworm changed from being a fortress town into the city it is today, isn't it?"

"Yes, yeeeees, right around when the dragon lady came to say helloooooooo. I thought maaaaaaaaaaaaybe it would go away if I slept it oooooooooooooooooff, but it slowly got woooooooooorse." The Giant God sniffed her nose loudly.

"Your face...is a little red, isn't it?"

"So, it is after aaaaaall? My head feels...kind of liiiiiiiiiight."

"Please excuse me. Hup!" Climbing the scaffold, Glenn put his hand on Dione's forehead. It was just a simple medical examination, but he was getting a workout.

The giant's bangs covered and hid her eyes. According to Dione herself, she was rather shy.

Glenn pushed her hair aside and felt her forehead. Her skin had a hardness to it that felt like tree bark. It seemed likely that her skin was strong and sturdy, instead of her bones, to support her immense weight. If that were the case, it was possible that the structure of her body might actually be closer to the plant-like monster races. Indeed, on closer inspection, Glenn could see that the green color of her hair was due to the moss growing on it.

The more Glenn knew about her, the more he felt like he understood what the tender-hearted Dione was really like on the inside. She was completely different from the brutal giants described in legends.

"Yup... It seems you have a little bit of a fever."

"Ooooooh, reeeaaaalllly?"

"Have you been experiencing any throat pain?"

"A liiiiiiiiiittle."

At first, Glenn had thought that Dione's voice had rumbled as if it were rising from the bowels of the earth, but now he clearly understood that it was due to nothing more than the pain in her throat.

"Hmmm... Sure enough, this is..."

"Doctor!" Sapphee shouted. "You should come down soon!"

"Yeah, I'm coming down!"

The scaffolding was quite tall. There wasn't much that could be done about that, however, as it had been built to match Dione's size. Glenn began carefully climbing down the scaffold's ladder. In total, there were four ladders attached to the scaffold. Climbing all the way up to Dione's face had been difficult, but going back down was hard work, as well. It was tough exercise for Glenn, who had gotten only a few hours of sleep thanks to the uproar of the previous night.

"...!"

"Doctor?!"

As he climbed down the ladder, the world suddenly swayed around him. He had lost his footing—by the time the thought had crossed his mind, his body had lost the support of the ladder. Glenn stretched his hands out toward it, panicking, but it was too late. It appeared his lack of sleep was going to harm him after all.

"Ngh!"

He could hear Sapphee's cries below. Glenn hoped for a second that an agile harpy would come and save him, but it was no use—there wasn't enough time.

Yet—

"Hwah?!"

"Oooooooh? That's dangerooouuuus, you know."

A cushion for his fall had appeared in midair. Held up by something elastic and flexible, Glenn had avoided violently crashing to the ground.

A mass of flesh had broken his fall—Dione's chest. That was how he had escaped his predicament: by being squished together between her ample breasts.

"Th-thank you very much! You saved me..."

"Noooot at all, I'm glaaaaaaaaad I was able to heeeeeeeeeeeelp."

Glenn had thought her skin was like tree bark, but...her chest seemed to be like a human's, a mass of elastic and bouncy fat. Her brown skin was soft, and Glenn's arm easily sank into it. Considering Dione's height, it wasn't surprising that the size of her breasts would also be completely beyond normal—and that someone of Glenn's size would be totally buried in her cleavage.

"Th-this...might be a little hard to escape from..."

"Doctor! How long are you going to keep that up?!" Sapphee shouted.

"I know, I know, but..." Glenn knew that it might seem from the outside that he was enjoying himself in Dione's cleavage, but in actuality, it was taking a great deal of skill to get himself free. Everywhere he touched felt like a bouncy cushion. He had nothing he could grab on to.

"Hwaaaaaaaaaaaaaaaaaaah, i-it tiiiiiiiiiiiickles!" Dione said.

"I-I'm very sorry. I'm going to move out of here, so—"

"Theeeeeeeeeeere we go."

A thick finger hooked the collar of Glenn's white coat. The digit was big even in comparison to Dione's physique. Despite its girth, however, it grabbed Glenn's collar with skill and lifted him up with no trouble at all. She wasn't good at moving quickly, but it seemed she could use her big fingers with unexpected delicacy and subtlety.

She was a colossal woman, but that wasn't her only defining trait.

Up until she had come to the village, Dione Nephilim had moved with sluggish steps as she walked. Apparently, she had been moving for close to two months. She would take a step, rest, then take another step and rest.

It was an exhausting story to listen to. When Glenn considered the frequency with which the earthquakes had been occurring when he arrived in the village, however, he realized that they were consistent with the timeline she had given.

But why had it taken her so long?

According to Dione, it was because she was worried about all the living things that might have been hurt by her passage. She would have hated to make a mistake and crush something with her feet, or frighten the animals of the mountain with any sudden movements.

She was a kind and gentle woman of great strength, but that wasn't all. Glenn thought her ability to carry her massive frame so gently and tenderly was incredible.

However, as these thoughts came to Glenn's mind—

"Agh?!"

"Huuuuuuuuh?" Dione said incoherently, and Glenn's body slipped through her fingers.

It seemed she had carelessly let him drop. Once again, he found himself diving into Dione's colossal cleavage. Not only that, but he fell even deeper in this time around, slipping into the ravine between her breasts.

The overwhelming mass on both sides of him felt like it was going to crush him.

"Oooooooh I-I'm soooooooooooorry," Dione said.

"I-It's okay, it's okay."

It has been said that it is a man's dream to be buried by a woman's chest, but in Dione's case the end result wasn't just a joke. Indeed, Glenn thought his life was in serious danger. It took everything he had to raise his arms up to the sky and seek help.

She was a compassionate woman, yes, but it seemed she also had a bit of a ditzy side to her, as well.

This time, Dione properly pulled him out from her chest and gently set him down in the middle of the village square. Glenn didn't think he would be forgetting that feeling of softness and body warmth any time soon. In fact, the experience, had been strongly engraved into his memory, thanks to how close it had put him to death.

"Thank you. You saved me."

"Doctor! Doctor!" Sapphee immediately slithered up to Glenn. "Honestly, Doctor! Before you fell into the canal at the Waterways, and now you're falling off of ladders! Just watching you makes me beside myself with anxiety, you know! So—what about your exam?"

"Oh, yes, I finished it without any trouble." Glenn looked up once again at Dione's face.

She straightened her clothes and cleared her throat with a cough. Her eyes were wide with wonder, waiting for the results of her examination—at least, that was the feeling Glenn got. It was hard to read her face with her bangs covering her expression.

"It's a cold, after all," he said.

"A cooooooooold... Just a cold?"

"Just a cold."

At Glenn's extremely normal diagnosis, a stunned expression appeared on Dione's face.

The Giant God Dione Nephilim had caused earthquakes and thrown a village into chaos all because she had caught a cold and gone to see the doctor. It was easy to see that her influence on the world around her was by no means ordinary.

Though the harpies' folktale hadn't portrayed her properly, her power nonetheless made her a special creature.

✖ ✖ ✖ ✖ ✖

Gigas had extremely slow metabolisms.

That was the conclusion Glenn came to from the exam he gave Dione. She had moss growing on her hair because of how exceedingly slow-growing it was. If she stayed almost completely still, her body expended only a small amount of energy, despite its size.

"That's how she supports her large body—with a low meta-bolic rate," Glenn said. "However, because of that, a cold can end up staying around for quite a while."

"Dr. Glenn, it's finished." Sapphee pointed to a tub filled up with hot water. It had originally been a tub the harpies used to wash themselves, so it was quite large. Glenn doubted he could lift it himself. In the hot water was an infusion of herbal ingredients, which gave it a dim color. "Will this even work on Miss Dione? It's just normal cold medicine."

"It should be fine. Miss Dione's body is on a much grander scale, but ultimately, gigas are just one species among many of giant monsters."

Glenn thought that Dione's species was possibly the primitive ancestor of modern-day giant monsters. She didn't seem to belong to some completely unknown species, neither human nor monster.

Whatever she was, monster evolutionary theory was his teacher Cthulhy's territory. All Glenn could do was heal Dione's cold—that and prevent her from catching another one.

"I suppose that means it's my time to shine, then? How I've been itching to get started." Standing there was Arahnia, fresh and lively.

Glenn had been telling Dione that it was important for her to protect herself against the cold. However, the clothes she wore were shabby and falling apart. Even if her cold healed, Glenn was sure that it wouldn't be long until she got another, considering her current state.

As such, Arahnia had volunteered to make Dione a new set of clothes.

"Heh, to be able to design clothes for the Giant God! My, my, my, I've used up all of my designer's luck, haven't I?! I'm going to boast about it without end once I'm back in the city!" Her ambitious words were, perhaps, misleading—but either way, Arahnia put everything she had into the hard task of making the Giant God's clothes.

"I have a limited amount of material," she said, "so making a whole outfit is out of the question, but, yes, that's right—I suppose I'll make an apron and a hat."

"Apologies for the inconveeeeeenience," Dione said.

The material was delivered by all of the harpies in the village. They were happy to prepare cloth and thread to help out the Giant God. Enshrined in the village square, it seemed the harpies of the village were really starting to like Dione. Glenn was sure it was thanks to her gentle personality.

"Now then, we..."

"...will attend to the Giant God's grooming."

Kay and Lorna brought with them a pair of pruning shears typically used for tree branches. It appeared as though they were going to trim Dione's hair, which had been free to grow indefinitely. Using the scaffolding that surrounded her, the two centaurs begin cutting Dione's hair, which had grown all the way down to her waist. It seemed that they were acting out of their concern for her, thinking that it was quite pitiable for a woman to have such a disheveled head of hair.

The two of them tied up Tisalia's hair on a daily basis, so they were able to cut Dione's hair quite quickly. Getting rid of the uncouthness of her haircut without changing its length seemed to be their intent. The two of them were very skilled, but dealing with so much hair was still a lot of work.

Someone brought up the idea of making Dione a pair of boots. Their size would be massive, of course, but it turned out that cobblery was also in Arahnia's territory. She supervised the creation of Dione's boots, commanding even the especially skilled village harpies.

Thanks to an idea Illy had, a clapper was installed in each of Dione's boots. Whenever she walked, the clappers would rattle and cause the animals of the mountain to avoid her steps. They would announce her arrival when she was visiting the village, as well.

In this way, everyone in the village worked together and did their best to do this and that for Dione.

"*Sniff*! I caused you all so much trouuuuuuuble, but you're still doing so much for meeeeeeeeeee." Good-natured Dione was deeply moved and looked on the verge of tears. "A looooong time ago I destrooooooyed the village just by moving a little, so I tried to be caaaaareful this time, but..."

"It's totally okay! It's tough to deal with everything that happens to you, after all!" Illy energetically declared from atop Dione's head. In the short time they had known one another, the two had become fast friends.

Hearing this, Dione again sounded on the verge of tears, loudly sniffing her nose. Glenn felt that her cold would still take time to heal, so he told Dione to stay in the village until she began to feel better. He was sure that Dione and the harpies would get along.

With this, Glenn had solved almost all of the problems in the village. The snow had stopped, and Glenn knew they needed to quickly head back to Lindworm. They had been there a long time and needed to reopen their clinic back in the city.

However, there was still one problem in need of resolution.

It was Tisalia.

Seated with her at a restaurant, the centaur seemed at a loss for what to do and had a frown on her face. In front of her was a heaping bowl of salad; she seemed almost desperate as she brought the vegetables to her mouth.

"Miss Tisalia, slow down a bit..." Glenn said.

"I can't just sit here without eating this!"

Glenn and Sapphee had descended the mountain without issue and returned to Lindworm. They had returned—of course—along with Tisalia pulling their carriage, and Kay and Lorna, too.

After getting back to Lindworm, the first thing Glenn did was invite Tisalia out to eat. During their trip up to the village, he had caused a lot of trouble for the centaur princess. First had been Kay's sprain, then her anxiety for Illy, followed by the difficulties with Arahnia—and then, after all that, Tisalia had taken up her spear to face the Giant God in combat.

Glenn was sure many of those problems wouldn't have been resolved without her. As such, he wanted to reward Tisalia for her hard work in whatever way he could. He couldn't agree to a marriage interview, so he had invited her to share a meal as a thank you.

The place they decided on was a restaurant managed directly by the Alraune Plantation. It was a restaurant with a very specific clientele, what with plant-type monster races serving the food and a menu consisting only of vegetables. It was quite popular among herbivorous races of monster.

"I had the resolution of a lifetime, you know!" Tisalia said.

Glenn thought that Tisalia's red face was most likely caused by her own embarrassment.

"I went to face the Giant God, I was even prepared to die... but in the end, all she wanted was to have you treat her cold! My resolve! My pride! What am I supposed to do?!"

"Isn't it a good thing that nothing ended up happening?"

"Well...yes, that's true...but!" Tisalia was in agony. She started to eat again as she languished.

She had been like this ever since they all returned from the village. Glenn, of course, understood the conflict going on inside her. She had resolved herself to a hopeless battle with the Giant God, yet she had returned home without crossing swords.

As a warrior, she didn't know how to let go of her pent-up will to fight without having an opponent she could do battle with.

The person she had planned to fight, Dione Nephilim, had received a wonderful hat and apron right before Glenn returned to Lindworm, made specifically for her. Made of copious animal furs, her new clothing was quite fluffy and looked very warm. There was no way Tisalia could have brandished her spear against Dione while the Giant God smiled bashfully at the presents she received.

"Aaarggghh... What should I do?!" Tisalia groaned.

Drinking the vegetable juice that had been brought to him, a charmed smile on his face, Glenn stared at Tisalia with her head in her hands. If she could vent her frustrations with just some grumbling and complaints, then Glenn was more than happy to lend an ear, and he had already planned on spending the evening with her anyway.

"Besides! There's something else I can't accept! Up there, by the ceiling!" Tisalia pointed her finger upwards.

"Don't mind me, Tisalia," came a voice from above.

Glenn had felt the same way regarding the presence above them.

He had planned on spending dinner alone with Tisalia, but for a while now, he had sensed the weight of someone's gaze watching him. It wasn't hard to figure out what was going on. From one of the beams near the ceiling, a single lamia hung upside down. With her long lower body and her tenacious tail, hanging was easy for her, but Glenn just couldn't take the situation calmly.

The same was true of the waitresses and other customers who were staring unabashedly, wondering what in the world the lamia in the ceiling, Sapphee, was doing. Glenn felt like he should apologize for her disruption, but Sapphee herself pretended not to notice the commotion she was causing.

"And just why are you dropping in on our date?!" Tisalia demanded.

"I should be asking you the same thing," Sapphee replied. "What exactly are your motives in going on a date with Dr. Glenn?"

"I simply accepted the personal invitation he gave me!"

Sapphee fixed a hard stare in Glenn's direction. He hadn't said a single word about them being out on a date, but, well—there wasn't much he could do if Tisalia had taken it that way.

Glenn could keenly sense the jealous Sapphee's immediate shift into a bad mood.

"Tisalia," Sapphee said with detachment. "Even with this affront, I still think highly of you. I think that your courage in deciding to face off against the Giant God was particularly wonderful." It was rare for her to praise Tisalia, but her words didn't have much of an effect on Tisalia's mood, dangling from the ceiling as she was. "If I were in your shoes," Sapphee went on, "I don't think I would have been able to do the same. I have respect for you, as a woman."

"In that case, won't you at least allow me to have a meal with the doctor?"

"That's exactly why I won't." Sapphee's eyes grew even more terrifying. "I have to be on guard and make sure a marvelous person like yourself doesn't cause Dr. Glenn to have a change of heart. To be perfectly clear, you're much, much more troublesome a person than Arahnia!"

"I'll thank you for minding your own business!" Tisalia said. "If you've accepted your defeat, then just say so!"

"I haven't lost—not yet."

The two women's quarreling was endless. In a panic, Glenn stopped both of them as Tisalia threw her fork and Sapphee feigned disinterest as she caught it in the air.

If things went any further, they would end up causing trouble for the restaurant.

"...Hold on, hold on. For now, how about we eat together, all three of us?"

At Glenn's words, Sapphee slid down from the ceiling, but for some reason, she settled beside Glenn so that she was facing toward Tisalia.

"This was supposed to be a wonderful date just for the two of us..." Tisalia muttered.

"How unfortunate. Now it's become three."

The two of them glared at each other like they were trying to keep one another in check.

Being flanked on either side by them was unbearable for Glenn. That said, even as they fought with each other, Glenn still felt a sense of friendship between them. The fact that they had both dropped formalities when speaking with one another was good evidence of this friendship.

"Infidelity is said to be a man's illness," Sapphee said. "We'll have to make sure you don't suffer such an illness—right, Dr. Glenn?"

"I'll make you catch the fever of love," Tisalia said. "Prepare yourself, Doctor!"

It seemed that the busy doctor of monster medicine wasn't going to have any time to take care of himself.

Afterword

HELLO, this is Yoshino Origuchi.

A whole six months have passed since my last work. I'd like to write with a bit more energy, but my thirties are just on the horizon, and frankly I've lost a little steam. Plus, my shoulders and lower back hurt. An occupational illness.

By the way, do you think centaurs get lower back pain?

I suppose the question is where a centaur's lower back is in the first place... Either way, it seems that the burden on their spine would be lighter than it is on a human's, so they probably don't have to worry about lower back pain at all.

What am I even talking about...?

I love arachne.

Or rather, I like spiders—scorpions, too. I also like crustaceans, like crabs and hermit crabs. The ecology of crustaceans is extremely interesting. I also love the huntsman spider because they catch those fast little black pests for me.

I'm not very good with tiny bugs or the black pests, so I think the house spiders that capture those kinds of things are wonderful.

The same is true of Arahnia Taranterra Arachnida, who was introduced in this volume. At first glance, she seems to have a complicated personality and is often misunderstood, but—she might just be an incredible, good person. That just might be the case with her, maybe?

I wonder which is more likely.

Despite being a new character, she was chosen to appear on the limited edition's wall scroll, so I hope you will enjoy more of the young arachne woman.

I went to a snake café and an owl café with a fellow author friend of mine.

I've wanted to own a snake for a while, but no matter what I try, I can't keep one in my house. So instead, my legs ended up carrying me all the way to a snake café.

It feels very good to touch a snake. They are soft and cool, yet also smooth because of their scales—it's a sensation that is very difficult to express. However, I *can* say this much: the feel of a snake is sensual.

In other words, snakes are erotic!

With that, time for my acknowledgments.

To the head editor, Hibiu-san. As always, I was able to continuously enjoy writing this volume thanks to the speed, precision, and excellence of your work. I always get too wrapped up in my passion whenever I start talking about monster girls, but I am truly grateful to you for listening to me without backing away from the conversation.

To Z-ton-san, the illustrator continuing his work from the first volume! Thank you so much for providing another special illustration for the wall scroll! The picture of Tisalia you drew for the cover is unbelievably cute, but I suppose that such is to be expected from such a well-known centaur illustrator.

To Kenkou Cross-sensei for their comments on the obi for volume two—thank you very much! I love Apophis-chan and Kraken-chan from your *Monster Girl Encyclopedia*. If this keeps up and I receive more such reviews from all of the other many nonhuman illustrators and artists, then surely the "monster doctor," form of nonhuman light novel will make a name for itself and take the industry by storm, won't it? Heh heh heh heh...

To all of the monster girl-loving writers who are always going along with me and to all of the monster girl and nonhuman manga authors—starting with Okayado-sensei and Shake-O-sensei—I truly thank you for everything. I don't think I'll ever stop talking about monster girls on Twitter with you, but please bear with me.

Thank you to my family for always casually giving me material to use in my stories, thank you to the proofreaders who always sharply point out all my mistakes—however small. And most importantly, to all of you—the readers of this book—I give you my biggest thanks of all.

In the next volume (if it happens)...

Dragons! Glenn's teacher! And cyclopes! I'm thinking it would be nice for the next volume to have those sorts of things in it.

—Yoshino Origuchi

About the Author, Yoshino Origuchi

I love monster girls—so much so that my writer friends and acquaintances have been calling me the "monster girl expert," or "Professor Monster" more and more lately. Since the first volume of *Monster Girl Doctor,* I've seriously started considering saying on my business card that I do monster girl research.

A favorite spot of mine is the snake café in Shijuku. I want to go again.

About the Illustrator, Z-ton

My name is Z-ton. I haven't been to a dentist in over twenty years. When I went in to get an examination as a bit of an experiment, though, they found the beginning of a cavity, which made me think for the first time in a while just how outstanding medicine is. Maybe there is a monster girl dentist in Lindworm, as well...?